SUNLESS

SUNLESS

A NOVEL

Gerard Donovan

THE OVERLOOK PRESS
Woodstock & New York

This edition first published in the United States in 2007 by
The Overlook Press, Peter Mayer Publishers, Inc.
Woodstock & New York

WOODSTOCK:
One Overlook Drive
Woodstock, NY 12498
www.overlookpress.com
[for individual orders, bulk and special sales, contact our Woodstock office]

NEW YORK:
141 Wooster Street
New York, NY 10012

Cataloging-in-Publication Data is available from the Library of Congress

Donovan, Gerard, 1959-
Sunless : a novel / Gerard Donovan.
p. cm.
I. Title.

Book design and type formatting by Bernard Schleifer
Manufactured in the United States of America
ISBN-13 978-1-58567-981-2
10 9 8 7 6 5 4 3 2 1

for my parents

As to diseases, make a habit of two things—
to help, or at least to do no harm

—HIPPOCRATES, *Epidemics* (400 BC)

SUNLESS

WHEN I WAS YOUNG a plane and then another one crashed into big towers and burned away the people in the windows, they fell and disappeared and everyone looked a long time for them. They were dots hanging out of the high windows, and I wondered what they were saying to each other, could they hear each other through the wind, maybe they said nothing and looked across the city. Then they were falling, they had their arms out to fly and left the television, and the buildings fell down too and rose up into smoke.

In Chicago we lived in a big room and had a balcony that looked across the lake. In winter it was frozen and gray with rocks and sticks caught in it for months. But in the summer people sailed up and down on the waves and it was full of red and yellow boats and people shouting. Then my father's job stopped and we had to travel west to another state to look for money. We came to a new lake that never changed and lived beside it in a house under a new sky that never changed.

The house sat on top of a small green hill. It had two chimneys and was long and narrow with six windows on each side, broken in places my father said he could fix, the timber floors and the walls, and he did. There was one small tree in the back garden inside the fence. When I stared at the branches from underneath they looked like the cracked lines around a rock in blue ice. A road beside the hill ran like a string out into the desert, and across that road from us was the wide and shallow water of the new lake.

My father's new job was like his old job. He cut wood in the yard of a large store closer to the city. Behind the sparks of the big saw, he wore his ear muffs, his goggles, an apron and gloves, away from the rest of the world. My father loved my mother and she loved him, she said it more than him. She was happy in the house and made it new, washed the windows and sang in them, she wore a red dress she got in the mail, she wore the smell of flowers that she splashed on her face from a bottle, she was in the kitchen, she was in the living room, she was moving between the rooms but never forgot where I was: she loved me too. When I went out to the garden her face was in the glass and she waved from every one, she was my mother in every window. She baked the bread in the oven, burned it so that it was crusty, and I ran off with the crust and shared it with the blue bird that lived in the branches of the brown, dry tree that got the sunshine first. Soon everything was fixed again, and the sun always shone in the evenings on the shallow waters of the Great Salt Lake and on the house where we now lived, my mother, my father, and me.

I was five years old when my mother's belly grew past the beginning of that summer. In July my father stuck his head into my bedroom and told me we all had a ship to launch. He held up a piece of curled wood that covered his face.

This ship, he said.

But it's only a bit of timber, I said.

He put it back in the plastic shopping bag and smiled. You'll see, Jimmy, come on.

After I was born they called me James first, then Jimmy for short, even though it was the same length, I counted the letters, and Jimmy even sounded longer, so why was it shorter. We drove along the road and I watched the lake move in and out of the windows, and after a mile we parked where there was a shore. My mother carried the blanket from the car to a dry part near the water. My father carried a jug of ice water. I brought a handful of ginger crackers over to them, and the three of us sat on the blanket and watched the sun move lower, and on the other side of the sky, the lights of the city went higher.

My father stood and rolled up his pant legs, saying to my mother, Mary, what do you think?

She said, It's time.

He rattled the bag at me. Now you'll see.

We waded out into the warm lake, it was only a few inches deep even after ten steps, and he reached into the bag and took out the wood and set it on the water and placed ten tea lights across it. My mother lit the wicks with matches, and the air around the ship filled with small suns.

I said, What's the name of the ship?

No name yet, she said. It has to be in the water more.

We stood and pushed the timber, following it as it floated out farther. The wet sun made my father's skin copper around his white shirt. He lifted me to his shoulders, how strong they were, his face smelled of rum, what he rubbed on it after he shaved. I moved my hands across the bristles and he laughed and swished his ankles around in the water; I clung to him and closed my eyes and could not smell enough of the salt, the cigarette smoke off his shirt, the vanilla of the candles.

My mother walked to the floating timber and lay on her back with her clothes on, holding her belly above the water. My father stopped jumping around and let me down and held my hand as we waded over to her. The timber touched her arm and bobbed and sailed against her belly as a small wind shoved the lights right and left, but they stayed lit. He was beside her in the waves, and for a moment I did not know what to do until she raised her hand and waited until I put mine in hers.

Come to me, baby, she said. You'll have a brother soon.

Out of the inches of warm water I looked at the clouds in the sky.

When is he coming? I said to the clouds.

She said, In a few weeks, won't be long now. He'll sleep in your old crib, wear your old clothes.

Are you going to give me away? I said.

They laughed together and she said, Jimmy, we'll be keeping you forever.

The water lapped my hands and legs and splashed into my mouth.

That's my very own boy who asked that question, my father said, cradling my head.

We lay in a row in the shallow lake. She smiled when he splashed her. The salt, she shouted. The sun kept itself in the sky for as long as it could until it touched the lake and was gone. Soon the flames on the wicks lit the whole night, and we went back to the house. I went to bed and said nothing about how a stick can turn into a ship and then a brother.

On a Saturday morning in August my father walked into the spare room and put into the closets the coats and books and bags and everything else in that room that had been on the floor. Some of the things emptied out of my room and filled the spare room. Next day he painted the walls, and the day after that I walked in and saw a crib in the corner, the crib I lived in when I was a baby, and I wondered why they needed a second baby when they already had one. My mother brought me shopping with her for clothes a couple of times, bags of them she piled into the car, and soon after when we got back to the house she flapped the clothes open, lifting them above her head and looking them up and down. I saw her smile and thought I heard her talking to the clothes, which was strange because there was nobody in them.

You were once this small, she said. I saw her face through the thin blue blouse. She laid the new clothes on the kitchen counter near a vase of flowers and folded them again and put them flat on her bed. My father came home and attached a string with angels hanging off it across the top of the crib. I wanted to ask who was coming, but my parents were so happy I decided not to ask, everyone seemed to know what was going on.

September came. My mother's belly grew big enough for two or three bellies. We spent more time inside the house because the first cold air of the season moved down the mountains and through the streets of Salt Lake City and west ten miles to where we lived. I often sat at my window and watched the city in the distance. One morning my father walked into the living room and slotted one of his films into the player, shut the blinds, and lit a fire to take the chill out of the air.

Then my mother said something. She reached out and touched my hand: Such a quiet little boy. I wish you would say more. Can you do that for me?

I said, My brother, where is he?

My father opened a big book and asked me to sit beside him on the couch. I did and saw that the book had pictures in it, one of them was a large thumb bent inside a circle, and he put his finger on it. The television screen floated in my mother's eyes as he placed the open page beside her belly.

That's where your brother is, he said. The pink thumb was my brother and the circle was what he lived in inside my mother.

What does he breathe? I said.

He breathes water. When he's born he'll breathe air, the way you did before him.

I said, Can we go to the lake?

My father went to the window and opened the blinds with the side of his hand and turned to her. She nodded and we drove to the shore again. The morning sun put its finger into the water and stirred some pale blue paint around and around. As he spread the blanket I knelt into the water and put my head underneath and opened my eyes, but the water stung and I came up fast. I felt something in there, maybe ten yards away, something in the current. I lay back so that my eyes and nose were above the surface and the rest of me floated underneath hearing words come through the water. More words, louder. I sat and my ears cleared to the sound of my father's voice:

Jimmy, I said you'll get a cold.

He was lying in her arms, and inside her there was a little lake where my brother was floating. So there were four of us all lying down.

A week came when she stayed home all the time and he called the house every hour, and every hour she picked up the phone and said, Not yet. Once she said: Paul, you worry.

But she worried too, the lines on her face moved across her forehead like ripples when the wind blew, and now the days were shorter and colder.

I tugged at her blouse, she replaced the phone.

I said, What's my brother's name?

She wiped her forehead and walked to the couch with big breaths and small steps. My brother and his little lake were heavy. I followed her and she sat, looked at the wall, closed her eyes and sighed.

What would you like his name to be?

But I don't know what he looks like, I said. If I gave him a name and he looks different, it could be the wrong name.

After a moment her face wrinkled into a laugh. When my father called again she told him what I said, listened to the phone a minute and then said to me, We will wait until we know what your brother looks like.

My father brought home a jungle of wood after work

and carried it into the house in four or five trips: a wood chair, a wood table, a small wood pen, and a new floor which he spent the following evening hammering down. This baby was important, I could tell, and while my room was not as nice, I did not mind at all. My father made the new floor, my mother sat with me watching the television. She held my hand to her stomach.

After she was snoozing I looked at my hand and waited for a while. The room was quiet, my hand was not tired but I wanted to move it a little. But I did not because it might frighten my brother with its shadow. The windows were open even though it was night, and my hand stayed waiting, but the baby did not move. I thought that maybe he was listening to my heart through my fingertips, his ear was pressed to her skin from underneath, his eyes closed, he was learning about me through my heartbeats. When I took my hand away my mother held her breath in her sleep, he had moved. It was clear to me now: all my parents could do was wait, the baby was the one deciding when to come out of my mother. He was comfortable swimming in all that warm water and not hitting anything and not getting lost. He might want to stay there. What if he didn't want to come out? And also, when the baby thought about himself, he didn't think of a name. What did he know for a name?

It would also be hard for him to see life on the outside and wondered how I could explain what air was and how to breathe it. He needed to know. What if the doctors and my parents forgot to tell him what to do. I went to my room and got some pages and wrote in crayon on top of a sheet of paper: *Air*. Then I wrote below it, *You pull the air in like a rope through your nose and down into your belly, then you push out the rope. You do this thousands of times a day. If you try to count, you will forget. If you stop, you cannot stop, so you have to keep doing it if you want to be alive.* In case my brother thought this was a lot of work, I said out loud that he didn't have to remember anything, it goes on even when he was asleep, and that when he ran around and played he would breathe a lot more air, there was enough for everyone.

He must have been able to see through the water.

I wrote, *You see when there are things and they are in your eyes. If you move your head or they go behind you, you do not see them. But they are still there.*

I wrote all of this in big writing on three pages and brought them to where my mother was sleeping. I placed the first one flat on her belly so the baby could read it, I shone a light onto the paper so the words stood out. When I put the second page on her belly, the baby moved, he was reading.

I wrote more and did drawings. I showed him how to feed the birds in winter. I drew a fence and a tree and a boy feeding the dots with wings on the ground. They sail out of the tree and other trees in other houses like seed when you throw the seed, isn't that funny, they mix happy around the food on the ground, and in spring, they sing notes from places you can't see because they are alive through all your windows in the summer until the freezing time again. This is magic and you are being born, brother, I said to him that evening in the pages that he read through my mother's skin.

She woke up. What's this, she said, holding the pages.

I said, I was showing him how to breathe.

She cried with water from her belly. After that, my father came home and gave me a present: a small black leather notebook and a pencil I could write with. I couldn't write much, I liked to make shapes, but I wrote down what was in my head and what I saw around me so that they lived for longer on the pages. My room was next to theirs and I knew I would have to move to give away my seat at the table and in the car and that my mother might not even notice me anymore. My brother was new and I wasn't, no matter what his name was. I was old now. They would take him to the lake and lie with him and play with him all day. I did not mind, he would need all those things. I planned the games we would play. I was happy for him until he could be happy for himself.

A Saturday and Sunday went by and still no baby. My father stayed at home on Monday waiting for my brother, but he was not coming out. From their bedroom I heard my mother tell him to go to work the next day.

One of us has to work, Paul, she said.

All that week and the next weekend, no baby, and on Monday my mother stumbled to the phone and shouted, Now!

She went to the couch and lay down and moaned. I ran back and forward, bringing nothing to nowhere. I said I would cut some bread for her. I was crying because she was moaning and I could do nothing. An ambulance was coming, she said, not to worry. The ambulance must have been lost for a while because it was thirty minutes coming and by the time it came my mother was groaning, and my dad got back at the same time, complaining about two ambulances and different companies and which one was covered by his insurance card. With all the busy people running around, I knew my brother must have been bursting to get out, there must have been something in there with him that made him so uncomfortable all of a sudden: nothing for a long time and now all he wanted to do was to get out.

My father walked me fast to one of the neighbors, Mr. Swan, who used to work but then got old and now stayed in his house all day watching television, he was a quiet man and nodded and patted the seat beside him. Then my father raced off to follow the ambulance to the hospital, his long legs in his black shoes running to the car and after the ambulance that was carrying my mother who was carrying my brother to the hospital.

Mr. Swan's house was very quiet. He turned to me. Would you like a cookie, I have different kinds.

Mr. Swan was asleep before I finished them, and two films and a lot of things for sale later I heard a car drive by while Swan was asleep. His eyes were half closed, and he never changed his position when he was awake or sleeping, so I had to say something before I knew which he was doing.

I walked to the window and said, They're back with my brother, and I ran out of the house and down the road and up the driveway and into the open door of the hallway, but I could not see my parents. I searched the bags on the floor for the baby, no baby in the first bag, searched the others. The house was silent. My father came out of their room at the end of the long wooden hall and lifted me up and squeezed me.

I said, Can I meet my new brother?

He said, Your brother stayed in the hospital with your mother.

How long, I want to see my brother.

Tomorrow, he said.

I went to the calendar on the refrigerator and rubbed out the big green crayon circle and moved it one box to the right and waited until the next day. It took all day to come, and then my father did not go to the hospital to get the baby. Instead a taxi came with a nurse and she took my mother into her bedroom, no baby, she stayed in the room with the door closed. I sat on my bed and kept my door open a little.

Twenty minutes later footsteps came along the hall and a hand pushed open my door.

My father smiled. There you are, we were wondering.

But his eyes were not smiling, and I began to cry too.

After my mother came back from the hospital she moved and spoke slowly. I wondered if she had a bit of the disease that killed my brother. She brought back a bag with two bottles of pills, she placed these in the cabinet above the kitchen counter. Every morning after that I saw her open the cabinet and reach inside for the pill-boxes, pick one tablet out of each and swallow them both with water. I saw them in the side of one eye while I moved the crayons across the page on the table. Those pills kept her quiet and took away the shaking and the crying. My mother loved me more again, held me tighter. Maybe the baby had been born inside me instead, and she was hugging him and not me.

In the evening she walked to the couch and sat with us in front of the television. We all stared at it. She pointed to the floor.

Paul, he would have been talking in a few months.

My father grabbed the knitted shoe off the ground and whispered, Mary, I'm sorry, I thought I took everything away to the spare room.

I was on the couch too but they did not see me or hear me because I was like a ghost or else my father was talking about me. The shoe that made my mother cry had a baby inside it that she could see but we could not.

When she went to bed I went to him and touched his arm, Did they count my brother?

My father looked at me. Count?

I thought of other words. Did someone count him?

He nodded a minute. When he looked up he said, Yes. He was alive. He was your brother.

I said, Where is he now?

He said softly, The angels took your brother.

So that was it. They could have left him with us.

The next morning, after my father went to work but before my mother got up, I stood on a chair and hitched myself up to the kitchen counter and stood on it and reached up for the cabinet door handle. It opened with a click and I reached into the dark and took them out. In my hand I read the labels:

L-O-R-A-Z-E-P-A-M. I said, *Lori's Pram*. Take one daily. No refills.

A-L-P-R-A-Z-O-L-A-M. *Alphie's Pram*, I said. Take one daily. No refills.

When I finished reading them I held out the pillboxes, one in each hand at arm's length, and said something to them. I said, The writing says my mother is to take you, it didn't say for you to take my mother.

I shook the two containers of pills. You can't have her. You can't have her.

My mother now spoke so little that I sometimes had to say things for her. When she sat on the couch in front of the television, I saw the programs she was watching open and close in her eyes. It used to be that she would ask me about my room and why it wasn't clean. It was clear: part of her had gone off to look for my brother. She lay on her bed a lot. I saw part of her head on the pillow down the hall. A month after my brother did not come I walked to my room and opened the door wide and began to clean. I hoped she would notice, but I heard her speak into a phone in her bedroom instead. Her voice was like a bird's feather.

Yes, Monday. A little better, but you know. Yes, I'm taking them. Yes, I will.

The summer went. Now it was the first cold weeks. I went to a school, a brown building with four rooms and a big window in each. The toys and the crib disappeared from the spare room. I was in the garden when I saw the Blue Jay pecking at the seed I threw. I was doing it because it was nearly winter and because my mother could not do it. It had its back to me, motionless in the middle of the grass at the seed, head cocked to one side, then dipped to the seed once, then sailed to the tree branch low after one flap, so wild and something I could never hold. An hour later it flew back to the ground. It was moving too slow.

The next day when I was walking along the side of the house on the concrete side path I saw it lying by the wall. The eyes were closed. I went up and it was not moving, was on its back, the little plump belly with the white feathers sticking up, the little eyes like saucers shut, a black line where the eyes shut, claws tucked in, the blue crescent on its head like a fan, what I had seen in the window as I watched the fan go up and down with his head, once or twice a minute, to the seed. Now I could touch it and the Blue Jay did not mind. The bird I watched that hopped around the ground was dead. Where had its life gone. I could hold it, but that was not fair, to hold it when it could not say no. I wrapped the bird in a tissue from the kitchen and brought it to my bedroom and kept it in the drawer. I slipped out of the house after midnight and walked out onto the bed of the salt lake and scraped out a hole with a stick.

I sat and looked back at the house of my father and my mother, the dark window for the room where they were sleeping at the other end of the hall. The stars were out above me. My brother did not have a name, so I would not answer to mine any more. Not even in the school. The bird was lost with my brother, the whole world was a lost thing.

My name was once James, then it was Jimmy. I decided to change it again.

I called myself Sunless, because the stars were bits of the sun that broke when it hit the ground and hid in pieces until the morning. When someone called me Jimmy, that word would enter my head and change into Sunless, my real name. No one would know.

When the morning came I was on my bed and opened my eyes wide on the blankets to let the light in. I waited for the sun to rise and make me bright. It never did. The weeks went by. In the months of dark I stayed Sunless, I had no other name I knew of or that came to me when I thought of myself. And even better, the name people called me changed to the right name after they spoke. I didn't even have to try after a while, it just happened by itself.

Silence grew like a plant along the walls and the windows of our house. Because my brother was not born alive, he stayed instead in our thoughts, like the electricity that runs in wires along the floorboards and turns on all the lamps but is never seen. That's how my brother lived in us, in me, and why I remembered him always.

A few months went by in the time of the pills, they lived in their little jars in the kitchen closet above the white counter that went to each side of the sink, the hard white counter, what you could stand on and reach the closet and not slip, because my mother kept the counter top dry and clean. I sometimes watched the brown door of the closet and wondered what the pills did when no one was looking, did they just lie there, for instance. She sometimes counted them, emptied them out into a pile and counted them back, it was nice for them to be cared for that much, I thought. I knew why she counted them. They were the days my brother was meant to be alive, each of them was a sun for that day, a round white sun to make her bright inside, so she had to be careful not to have a day when there was no pill. What would my brother live under then?

I went to the school three days of the week, the other days we stayed at home to read the books because of the terrorists. Everyone went home after school. The playground was full only when the children walked across it in the morning and walked back to their parents' cars in the afternoon. I wanted to play with the other children but their parents were always waiting on time. It was safer and allowed more time for families to spend together, the school principal said. I had never seen anyone play in it, it was too exposed, she said. She opened her arms wide when she said exposed, that's how I knew the word. I did not know what all the other children did at home. They never talked to me about what they did. I wanted to tell them about my brother. But their parents were always waiting and blowing the horns after school and waving at them to hurry.

Most of the days my mother came for me, sometimes my father. One day she did not come at all for an hour and I was waiting in the classroom by the big window. I was the only one left, the rest of the children were gone, and I watched the empty playground. The wind ran around on the glass. The window had a crack running along the side. I sat and waited for my mother, looked through the glass for the car, and her in it.

My eyes got caught in the crack. Maybe the sky was broken and not the window. I made a list in my head of what can fall out of a sky: rain, snow, wind, planes, sunshine, birds, people. The handle of the window was in my hand, I pushed it and the big window opened, a big creak. I stepped onto the steel frame. The ground outside was a long way down because there were concrete stairs running down to the basement. I stood on the ledge of the window and looked down. I could line ten of me head to toe up the wall to the window. I let one hand go and I almost went out and gripped the frame with my other hand. What the falling people from the high windows thought about—they must have been real thoughts.

I had no real thoughts. I could not forget my brother, I could not make the sun come up in me. It was dark inside me. My mother had the pills to make her insides bright. I did not.

In the film of the planes and the buildings, I remember seeing one man fall down between them on his own. His arms were spread out, he was facing down. What could he see? What was in his pockets? What he did when he was little, is that what he thought. What he played at and what toys he owned. His sisters and brothers and father and mother. Or when he was little and something he saw then. Did he have money in his pockets, did he have enough money, could he give it to someone, could he talk to other people in the lower windows, did he talk to only himself? He did not say anything, I saw that he did not. What was below him was a longer way down than this window. His shoes were polished, he had a shirt and a tie. His was falling a long way, his jacket was full of the wind and it made wings. Did he have a brother who would not see him again.

I was able to stand straight and look ahead of me. The ground was a long way down and I would stand here for a while. Out of nowhere, two hands grabbed my hips and pulled me back. The voice in my ear said, Okay, and I was lifted down to the classroom floor again.

I'm glad I caught you, the voice said.

It was not my mother's voice, not my father's.

A hand closed the window.

Now let's go to my office.

I walked in the woman's hand until we went into her office, it was crowded with books and pictures of red and black children playing on the walls. The woman told me to sit down at the desk, and she sat on the other side. She reached behind her and opened the fridge door and showed me some ice cream. She put two big lots of it on a saucer and stuck a spoon into it.

It's vanilla ice cream, she smiled. Would you like some?

I thought it was for her, she was very big and wore big clothes and a lot of big long hair and had a lot of lipstick on her mouth and long nails on her fingers. She smiled when she saw me looking at the ice cream, and she slid it to me.

It's very good, she said.

I took the saucer and took out the spoon and put the ice cream on my tongue.

Isn't it good, she said.

Yes.

Now, Jimmy, I have a question, she said.

I looked at her and tried not to look at the ice cream, I was hungry.

She smiled with big teeth: Have you ever been tested?

No.

Have you ever been to a doctor who asked you if you were happy?

No.

Or if you were sad sometimes?

No.

She leaned across the table. I pulled the ice cream closer to me by the same length.

She said, You've never been tested? She made her hands move as if she was drawing. Have you ever answered questions about squares and circles and what they looked like to you?

No.

Another spoon of the ice cream, it went over and under my tongue. I saw her looking at it, I knew she wanted some of it.

That looks tasty, she said.

I kept my hand on the spoon: It is.

She hunched her shoulders and put her head to one side: You are such a lovely little boy, you have such pretty little dimples.

I let my eyes drop to the ice cream in case she put a hand on it.

My name is Brie, she said. I am the school counselor. I did want to speak to you before this, but your father wanted to wait. And today I have to lift you away from an open window. So I'm going to speak to you now. Is that okay?

Yes.

She put a finger on the saucer and rubbed it. I bet you'd like some more.

Yes.

But first I have a question. You are so pretty, your little mouth is so pretty.

I said nothing back. She said that because there was ice cream in it.

My question, she said, is this: Do you ever feel sad?

No.

As if the world is pressing down on you? She lifted her very big arms and pulled down something invisible over her head.

I looked up. The sky pressing, you mean?

She nodded. Yes, the sky. That's what I meant.

The sky does not do that.

She looked sad and said, Not even a little?

No.

So you're not taking anything?

My mother takes everything.

Your mother is on medication?

No, she's taking pills. My father calls them pills.

She shook her head and her hair waved and her nails tapped the desk. No, that's not correct. We say 'medication' or 'drug therapy.' Saying pills—she hung two fingers around the word—is derogatory.

She must have meant to put the fingers around that last big word she said and missed, because I never heard it before. The ice cream was gone and I would have liked more.

Who makes the tests, I said.

Makes?

The tests you talked about.

She said, That's an interesting question. Experts make them. Her fingers went in the air again around 'make.' She pointed to her head: They measure what is going on in your head.

My head or your head?

This is about you. Then she whispered: Are you really happy? Are you happy, are you sad? Has your father or mother ever touched you in different places, your arms—she touched her arms—your belly—she touched her belly—or anywhere else? She pointed at the floor between her legs.

I tried to look where she was pointing.

I said, What is in the tests? What are they made of?

She sighed and reached into the fridge and put more ice cream on the saucer for me. I took the spoon and bent to some of it.

She said, We need to know.

Her voice was not friendly and I wondered if I was taking all the ice cream and she was getting mad. Then she should stop giving me the ice cream.

She clasped her hands in front of her. Do you have issues?

I think she meant to say something else.

Yes, I miss my brother, I said. I miss him a lot.

No, no. That is different. I mean you—what do you feel when you are not thinking of your bother and just doing other things?

I am always thinking of him. Can I tell you about my brother?

She said, Do your mother and father talk about him?

No.

Why not?

I don't know.

She shook her hair slowly. That's denial. You must know about your brother.

I said, Maybe I will see him again.

Listen, Jimmy. She made a V of two fingers and grabbed one: First, your brother is dead, he is gone, and that is sad. Second, he will not be coming back, not in this life, but maybe in the next life.

How do you know?

Because I am a psychologist. Brothers do not come back, they don't just re-appear. Your brother is in a better place. You need to know that. We need to figure out what you should be taking to help you.

She ran out of fingers and grabbed the first one again.

No medication at all?

No.

That's really sad, she said. Because you are missing

out on so much, if only we could get you tested. If only your father—

You can ask him, I said. I don't take any of my mother's pills.

That's not—she shook her head and sighed. You have a condition that made you stand at that window, and we can cure it and you'll feel better. You were standing by the window about to do something.

I was thinking about falling people. I wasn't going to fall myself.

See, she said. See? We have to address this. This is very serious.

I said, What falling people think when they are falling. That is what I was thinking.

You were thinking of falling? She nodded a very loose head. And your parents left you alone after school? And again she nodded. I almost started nodding, but I shook my head instead.

No, I did not want to fall. I was wondering about planes that fall out of the sky and buildings.

Her eyes opened wide. Of course. Yes, the buildings and the planes. Long ago, September 2001. Terrorists came in planes and caused people to fall out of the sky. So it's trauma.

Why couldn't the terrorists fall out of their own sky?

Her eyebrows tilted. What?

Why did they come out of our sky and not out of their own sky?

Because they hate us. She folded her arms and sat

back. Her mouth was thin and pressed hard.

She said, They hate what we have, our freedom.

I said, Can they take anything for the hate?

Nothing. And they will be back, she said. Only a matter of time.

I said, How do you know? You said my brother wasn't coming back.

She looked out her office window and watched something and turned to me: Your mother is here.

I stood at the window and saw my mother's car parked. She was already inside. I walked out of the room and followed the sound of her voice along the dark of the hall: I could find her by the sound of her voice. She was speaking to someone.

I saw her through the crack of the open door, sitting in a seat with her head on the desk.

Where are you, she said. I wish I knew where you were. Why did you leave me?

I did not see anyone else in the room.

I am here, I said. I didn't leave you.

She jerked her head and her eyes were full of tears and happy, and she saw me and blinked until her eyes were tears and not happy.

It's you.

She held her hands out to me and I moved to her.

I said, Were you asking where I was?

She shook her head. Yes.

She held my hand and said, Your father is strong, do you know that?

Yes.

The red lines on her face ran through her eyes. The crack in the window, I thought, meant the sky was breaking. Maybe those plane crashers were coming back after all. We should hide.

Can we go home? I said.

Let's get out of here, she said.

We walked through the hall and into the sun of the concrete yard. The principal walked behind us, and she spoke while we stood under the different white recording cameras at the front door of the school.

It's a pity we can't have the children playing in the open. She put her hand across her eyes in the sun. It's safer for the children if they play at home. We let the last part-timer go this week. She glanced into the sky: Can't see them, but they're out there.

I followed where she was looking. It was blue and flat, not a cloud, not a sound.

Where are they? I said.

She laughed, If we knew that, we wouldn't have to look for them, would we? We wouldn't be in such danger, would we? Why give them a soft target like children? My, what an interesting little fellow you are. She twisted her hands. They say an attack is imminent. Been saying it for weeks.

My mother took me across the empty yard. A bird flew over the yard and sang on the sill of a window.

When we sat in the car my mother spoke to the steering wheel:

We shouldn't have come here.

To the school?

No, here. We should have stayed in Chicago. None of this would have happened. I know that now.

A weed slapped the windshield as we drove out of the school yard. The principal was standing under the cameras. We turned for our house. We passed other houses. The streets were empty. The cafés were closed.

At home we turned on and watched the television, it flashed bright in the living room. The newsreader said, We have a newsflash: Five people dead in a plane crash in Nebraska. The weather is sponsored by Pharmalak. How will you feel tomorrow? At Pharmalak, we care. What's happening with the weather, Mike?

We'll all be feeling a little chilly tomorrow, Diane.

Is that right? Better wrap up tomorrow, everyone!

I watched the television with my mother, she gazed at it and the flashes did not cause her to blink. On another program they showed the planes smashing into the tall buildings again, the yellow flames in the blue sky, and then people talked about it around a table. I thought it was news when I saw it on the television in Chicago. Now they were still showing it on this television. So it might have happened before I was born.

That evening two young men in suits visited the house and told my father they had a spiritual message. My mother was watching the television when he let them in. He was tired from work but he listened, nodding his head at their explanations and diagrams, and when they were finished he told them that he had a message for them, that he would bang their heads together if they came back. After he went to work the next morning the door knocked and it was the two men again. It was strange that they came when he was only two minutes gone. They talked to my mother instead, they gave her a big book, and she hid it. She read it for hours and a week later she said not to worry, that we would see my brother in the next life, there was no need to be sad.

But she still took the pills and they still took her.

A year and then twelve years passed like a bandage.

My father worked his job at the lumber yard, my mother stayed at home. She tried a job here and there, but they never lasted. I was finished with school. I made an airplane out of the diploma that came in the mail and threw it—watched it slow to a hang above the tree in the back yard and land upside down on a curled branch and flutter in the sun and the wind for a couple of days before it broke free and blew away. For the past year I worked four hours a day at a convenience store on the service road off the road a couple of miles out west into the desert, a square building with the cigarette and beer prices daubed in huge orange letters on the windows. I cycled there and worked the early morning shift, which was the best time because you had the same people coming in and you knew what was going to arrive through the door. One man always stood in the aisle, read through the newspaper in his gloves, every page of it, and then bought the news he'd just read. The woman in a headscarf smiled and asked me if I had witnessed anything today, and when I stared at the cash register as I always did, she bought the same brand of milk and left. The third regular wasted no time: entered the store as if being chased, went briefly through the aisles and up to the counter, produced the soda he put under his coat and touched one brand in the rack of cigarettes, saying, Those. He never named the cigarettes, he never made eye contact. The owner was a Pakistani who spoke only the words he had mastered without any connecting words. I learned to fill in the ones he couldn't speak for him. I could tell he trusted me because he left me alone in the store after a couple of months.

One day my father came home with a strange cough, and in a couple of weeks it had grown in him like a vine that ran little wires through his lungs and also through the house, through the walls. I lay at night in bed and listened to him struggle. He got a stomach ache that made dull spoons of his eyes, very soon he looked thirty years older than forty-two. Time moves differently in sick people, it slows down or speeds up.

I drove him to a doctor who put a scope to his chest and made him breathe deeply, tapped him here and there like a wall before the nail is hammered in. That doctor then referred him to another doctor, and my father made the appointment straight away because he had a job and health insurance. The second doctor had him tested and scanned. The results came back in a couple of days. When that doctor called and asked my father to come to his office to pick up the results as well as a prescription for medication the doctor said he needed to take, I knew that the vine must have shown up somewhere on the map. Maybe it was the vine of silence after my brother died. I held my father's pill-boxes in my hands and urged them on. They looked like better pills to me because he was the still the same man to me, a happy man after taking them, unlike what happened to my mother.

The second doctor referred him to a specialist who said there was an operation to remove portions of his stomach and lungs, but my father said that he would first like to give the medications more time to work. At home at the dinner table he shook the pills at his ear like dice or castanets to make light of them. After two months he began taking days off, the lumber people hired a part-timer to fill in for him. How much it hurt my dad to lose his space in the yard: when he was alone with my mother I heard him talk about the insurance, that we couldn't let it drop. The words drifted along the walls and into my room as if searching for more ears.

After three months he missed so many days at work that he was fired. I found the store manager's letter in the morning post and handed it to him while he watched a movie, Humphrey Bogart steering a boat down a river with a cigarette in his mouth. My father opened the envelope that shone in the light of the screen. I saw him read the page, fold and slip it into his breast pocket.

He smiled over to me. Well that story's over, he said. It's for the best. You take care of your mother for me.

He had just told me that he was going to die and what I should do after that. His job was gone. His health insurance was gone. Some days later, after the pain went down a little, he sat in his armchair and prodded numbers into the telephone to respond to an advertisement for research volunteers he saw in the back page of the *Salt Lake City Tribune*.

My mother floated in and out of the living room, opening the windows for the air, it made him feel better. Her eyes were red as if she used them for more than seeing, as if she had stuffed every bad thing in the world into them and then tried to see despite those things anyway, which can't be done. She did everything living people do but was missing her insides. She waited until he put the phone down and he held his arms out to her: she bent into them and he said,

They say I can go up there to Park City. I may get accepted into a clinical trial.

They embraced. I stepped away into the hall, relieved that there was some kind of happiness in the house.

In the kitchen my mother and I spread a map under the kitchen light. We'd been to Park City a few times, last drove through it on the way to Missoula, Montana, some summers before. It was a mountain resort and the home of the pharmaceutical company Pharmalak. We underlined the route in pencil and drew a small circle around Park City.

I'll drive, I said. She slipped her hand around my arm and tightened it, a wordless word that meant hope: him getting his life back, and she hers.

I went to bed thinking about hope, what it was and where it came from. The loss of my father, what hope could stop that now? Yes, hope had appeared for certain in our house, but I saw it as something that came before despair, in that order. I saw it mask the rapidly decaying features of my father. It was not malevolent, just blind to what lay before it, a walking stick poking at the dark for direction.

After breakfast in the morning my mother and I helped my father out to the car and eased him into the front seat. She put the picnic blanket over him, and for a moment I thought how better it would be to go to the lake instead and spend the day there. What was the point.

It was a forty-minute drive to Park City, a right turn and two miles along the valley between mountains until the gigantic cream walls of the Pharmalak building rose out of a slope to our right.

It's a damn castle, my father said.

It was clear that someone had money here. Five long rows of windows glistened up to the roof with battlements, four towers built into the corners with turrets, a flag fluttered off each. To the right the roof curved steeply to a larger tower with a single window in it: that would be the king or the watchman. We pulled up to the wooden entrance door and helped my father out. He waited on a bench while I parked, and then we walked together across the carpeted lobby, past a fireplace and into a café divided into twenty or thirty private booths with coats of arms on the walls and leaning torches with bulbs instead of flames. On the wall a television said something about people forgetting things and what they could take for it.

A woman wearing a white coat and a clipboard arrived at our booth. We filled in the forms, she drew his blood. Because of his condition, there was no waiting beyond a blood test and the results. The woman came back in less than an hour and held his hands. Her face said no before she said no. That was that.

We drove down the mountain. It was high summer, the middle of July, and he asked me to open the windows and turn on the air conditioning at the same time, and the wind blew the cool blue sky around the inside of the car. Near Kimball Junction he said we should pull over. I helped him to the edge of a meadow as my mother spread a blanket and we relaxed in the morning air and listened to the birds sing. He lay on his side and closed his eyes and let the sun stretch warm on his skin, she went beside him and hugged him, then we had some sandwiches. I rolled onto my back and watched a cloud find a tree in the center of the meadow. It made no sense to me, how helpless an entire hospital was and all the doctors inside it. At six we packed up and drove away. My father looked at the passing fields, the meadows, the flowers that leaned in bunches over the road.

He signed on to a different type of health insurance. Because he had waited more than one day before switching companies, they said no to everything because he had already been sick, it was pre-existing, they said. He told me he was thinking that maybe an operation was the best thing to do after all, but after four or five months he went fewer times to the specialist because he could not afford him. A month after that, my father couldn't afford any doctors at all. I passed his bedroom and saw him sitting in a chair by the bed, his head in his hands, saw the gray terror on him.

He decided to get the operation done, but his new insurance company told him he had no coverage for pre-existing conditions for two years. Then it would take approximately three months to process the paperwork once he did make the request. The specialist said that perhaps he might feel well enough to get a job, any job that provided health benefits, and then he could proceed with the operation, since everything was ready and the procedure would probably cure his condition. There was every reason, the specialist said, to feel confident.

Using the rest of the family's savings, my father enrolled in a health plan where the doctors were online and the drugs arrived in the mail. The medicine cost more money than the rent. Soon enough I heard the same bodiless words float from their room to mine.

I'm selling the mandolin for this month's premium.

She would not let him, she said, sell that antique mandolin. He had played to her on it before they were married.

I listened to those floating words. Though he'd stopped smoking a few years before, my father's voice was a pack of cigarettes: they liked his body so much they made little tubes in their own image in his lungs and infiltrated his breath with the wheeze of their own throats. I worked more hours to help with the prescriptions, the hundreds of dollars they sucked out of our pockets. I ended up paying for the household food too, but I could not keep up with the pills, not with forty hours of work a week, not with eighty. When the money ran out, even the mail pills stopped, which is when the pain grew, layers of long pain, pain lined up around the corner and all the way to the end of the street, pain that talked to itself while it waited to get into his body.

Eleven months after he had first come home with the vine growing in him, my father's body wrapped itself entirely into wires, his flesh sank to bone. I held his hand every evening before bedtime, underbrush on a forest floor. I wanted to rip the vine out of him, but if I did, nothing would remain. I could have gathered and carried him as he did me when I was a child and when we were on the lake and it was summer, but nothing remained of that life. When the moans became one moan, we rushed him to a hospital, where one morning close to noon, he died.

I did not remember the men who came to the mortuary to put my father into a funeral hearse, or my mother and me walking behind it for a few hundred years, or was it yards, both dressed in black, until we got to the mortuary chapel, where I stood outside a holding room as she sat with him and cried as quietly as she could. I did not remember entering that room and standing there, looking into that box, he and I alone. I did not remember spending a minute waiting, how his forehead was a white wax stone, or walking away, the hearse with his body in that casket turning for the hospital, for the mountains, not going down into the earth but up to where he had promised it for research. My mother and I walked around the neighborhood for an hour and said nothing, and then we went home. I did not remember because I did not forget. His work friends came to the house, and one of them handed my mother his goggles and apron.

She made sandwiches.

When the people were gone and we were alone she showed me the book the two men in suits gave her after my brother died.

She said, We will all be with each other in the afterlife, you don't need to grieve your father, you will see him again. See, I'm not sad. She smiled under her red eyes and went to bed.

I watched the night away in television until the sun rose, then I went for a walk. No work for me that day. I went for walks every few hours, crossing into the streets behind the hill that led to other houses spread out behind us and off to the sides. My father was detained in a steel room: steel counters, steel gurney, steel instruments, steel floor, all steel, a planet of shiny gray steel, atmosphere of antiseptic. The charts of the human anatomy, bones, tissue, organs. A whole body taken out and hung up on the walls, the illustrated insides of a man. Now for the curious students—the first real cut into real flesh. Above them, over the metal dissecting table, a bulb whose light slants to a catch basin, a drain, a faucet, tongs, cutting blades, spiny sutures with needles, steel washed and scrubbed.

When I got back to the house again I expected to see him in his armchair reading a newspaper or watching the flashing screen. That's the thing about dead people. Your brain won't let them go and keeps on the lookout for them. Dead person coming down the stairs, dead person waking you up, dead person bringing you to school, dead person watching television. Dead person. My dad.

The house had one person less, but it filled with other voices.

Before the life insurance money came the letterbox filled with bills and the bank started to call and leave messages saying they must insist that sums be paid, thirty days, sixty days late, machines talking messages with the name of the account and the amount owed filled by a human voice. My mother went to the doctor's and came back with more of the usual Lorazepam and Alprazolam. She took one pill of the usual two each morning and night: they were the sun and moon of her day. She reached under the bed where she kept that book, though no one would object if they saw it now.

In sixty days the life insurance money came to replace my father, a thin envelope that held the money that could have saved him. The bills stopped coming, the phone stopped ringing for money. Silence and peace came down upon us in the house where my mother and I lived.

Brian Willow was one of my teachers from my time at the school. He was a willow tree, his eyes and jaws hung about his features. His mouth was set in a line of a poem under his forehead of white hair, his shoulders were coat hangers for the jacket that hung past his hips. In his office he kept socks and two books in a brown bag on the shelf, I saw a sock hang out of it and two black shoes on the top shelf when he turned the dial on the radio beside the brown bag. Bach, he said, and waved a pencil to the piano music that came out. Behind his chair what he wore to class on cold days, a maroon military coat with a hood and brass buttons from 1760. His finger was a hook for the mug that he poured into when he read some Blake and Keats to us one morning, about ten it was, and showed us the drawings of Mr. Blake, his lamb in a red shade. In the Keats poem I saw the Greek vase where the ancient boys chased the ancient girls but didn't catch them, leaning to a kiss, that's where it stopped, leaning to the kiss. Mr. Willow walked the aisles of the class reading these long verses, coming to a stop by sliding one foot out and feigning surprise at the last line.

I went back one day to see him after my father died. I don't know why. He was leaving his office.

He looked at me a moment in silence and said, Hello Jimmy. My wife is sick, but let me drive you home.

We went out to his car, a pink Ford parked away from everyone else at the far chain link fence. He walked around it three times, puffing a cigarette and blowing the smoke before opening the door. He did all that, he walked around the car and touched all four corners with the smoke trailing out of his mouth. As we drove along the road out to where I lived, he laughed.

I have an echo, he said.

What's that?

You know. I do things a certain number of times and I can't stop. I walk around the car, I check things, I go round in circles. You saw it in class, you all did. I saw you watching me just now.

Can you take something for it, I said.

He frowned and stuck the dead cigarette into the ashtray, turned down the harpsichord music from the tinny speakers.

Why would I do that?

To stop the repetition.

He lifted a hand off the wheel. And what would I do then? Simply get into the car and drive? And taking medicine, refills—that's repetition.

I said, I don't understand.

He said, You see, it's a gift. You have to look on it as a gift.

He turned the music back up. To hear him I had to cup my hand at the ear.

Now he lifted both hands off the steering wheel: I have two arms that look exactly the same, two legs, two eyes and ears. It's a rhyme, repetition is everywhere in nature, I just got a too much of it. What about you, Jimmy?

My father died, I said.

He nodded and looked at me and said nothing. It

was the best thing. The repetition must have been a gift, to repeat a silence into another silence over the tires on the road as we drove. When we passed the lake on our right, he asked how much more it was.

Another five minutes, I said.

What are you going to do? he said.

Maybe go to college or not, work, I don't know.

He said, Not college. Learn a trade, don't hang around here, make some money and keep yourself busy.

For that he had turned the knob down, but the harpsichord went loud again near the end of the sentence, and again I had to strain. He would have traveled more himself, he said through the noise, but his wife was sick a lot, though she was a great companion.

And anyway, no one else will have me, he said.

Could you repeat that? I said.

You see, he stabbed the smoke, that's way too smart for college. Go out and learn how to bang some nails together and put some measure into the week, look forward to Fridays. In a college every day is the same blur of books and bullshit.

He waved the cigarette across the windshield, conducting the music of the smoke.

You know where echo comes from, he said. The story of Echo. How long do I have?

I pointed, I'm up ahead there.

Brian Willow stuck another cigarette in his mouth and blinked in the flash of the lighter.

Echo, he said, was a woman in ancient Greece who could not stop talking. Compulsive. One day she was at it again, yakking to Hera, and in the background two captives escaped because Hera was caught up in the talk.

In a rage Hera put a spell on Echo. She said, You cannot speak any more. You can only repeat the last word that is spoken to you.

Willow slapped the wheel. This of course, you know, was devastating to Echo. She went away for good, living alone in the rocks of canyons, and when anyone walked in among the rocks and happened to say or call a few words, they heard the last word repeat as she kept calling it back to them.

She faded into the rocks. That was the last trace of her, she became a voice.

For the last minute of the drive I thought of last words, what my father's last words were to me and I to him. Where I saw him last. What he wore. What I was doing.

I did not know.

When I was at my door, Willow leaned across the seat and called out the car window: You lose as much as you loved. It comes back, Jimmy.

He tore off in sand and dust as I waved to his streaming face in the smoke clawing out of the pink car.

In the house, I thought about what he said. I thought those pills must be good if she could take them for so long. We had both lost the same things but by different names: her son was my brother, her husband was my father, and surely my mother and I should therefore share the same remedy, at least for a while. I wanted to feel nothing. That too was a feeling. In a sense the pills must have taken away her loss and replaced it with a different loss, a condition of general emptiness.

So one night after she went to bed, I tried one.

No one would miss one pill.

At about midnight and I thought I was asleep when I sat up in bed, went to the window and looked outside. It was freezing but I had left the window open for the fresh air. I parted the blinds, and the moon splashed cool light onto the desert mountains and the dirty white salt crystals that stretched for miles over the dry bed of the Great Salt Lake. I turned my face to the city and ahead to the shallow water around Antelope Island. Nothing moved until pinpricks of light shone near the single road out to the Nevada border a few hours away.

I knelt on my bed, unsure if I was asleep or awake or somewhere in the middle. My thoughts seemed off to the side. Come back thoughts. I liked the feeling of no feeling. Stay away for a while, do that. I watched as a light floated across the salt, someone on a long drive to somewhere, joined by another light that seemed to float away and back. The breeze let me stay asleep, and sleep showed me pictures that I could look at in my dreams: those lights out on the dry part of the lake, the white crystal bed, they must be candles. I leaned on the window sill in the cold, but that cold was absent suddenly, something lifted off my skin, and strangely I was able to see those shapes in more detail—a woman, a man, shadows that wandered across the salt. I was on the salt myself. And when I walked close to them, my heart raced and skipped and jumped because I was afraid they might see me dreaming them and approach me in my sleep. I saw the faces of my parents, and staring out at me from between them, my face.

I lay down onto the covers and went on my side. Or I was already asleep and only dreamed I lay down.

The next morning, when I was getting my mother her morning dose, I slipped another pill into my mouth to layer the first, to keep the momentum going. I did that for a few days as each day crossed namelessly into the next. Could have been days, could have been weeks. The pills kept me pressed down and out of any place. Sometimes my mind seemed attached to my brain at the end of a thin string. I was on one side of the room, what I felt was on the other side of the room, this is what I mean. Under a heap of blankets I waited for the shadows and lights that filled my dreams. One night I opened the windows wide to stay awake and the room filled with white pale light from the salt and lit my lungs. I burned a candle and put it on the window sill to warm my face while I watched the dark. To anyone driving past I'd look like a spirit, a face in a long night with no body.

If they knew me they might say, That's Jimmy, he has no body. He puts himself at the window to be seen, even in a dream.

My mother stayed most of the time in her room after my father's death. She spoke less too, walking around the house like a body anonymous to itself, and she touched fewer things, maybe a glass for water, the handle of a closet for a cup, the lid of the bread bin. Often I didn't know she'd been out of her room until her door closed when she returned to it. She was vague even to herself. The less there was of her, the less there was for her to feel.

On one of those nights a door closed somewhere in the house. I left the window and knocked on her door.

Her voice: Yes.

My voice: Can I get you anything.

The voice returned: I'll see you in the morning, Jimmy.

After a click her room went dark under the door. I went back to my own bedroom and the window. When I looked out, two lights flickered down by the highway near the water, the silence mortared across the sky and the mountains, the yellow blur of Salt Lake City to the east, and the towering Wasatch mountain range, the broken surface of the moon, endless on nights like this, a place you put a foot down and were the first. I shivered in my socks and coat and the cap I wore to keep the breeze off my head.

But first I took another pill, the first time I'd taken

two in one day: two Lori's Prams. Take two just this once.

At the window again, floating, my organs drifting inside in a slow tide, I put my head down for a second. I thought of the lights and then my brother, wondered where he was. He couldn't have disappeared those years ago, never saw a sight of him, there had to be something. His complete absence here was proof of his presence somewhere else. Why hadn't that simple truth occurred to me before? And all this time I thought I'd lost him. Where do unborn children go? I drifted too along with my insides back and forth along the window sill like a ship moored on loose rope waves that stretched to hold the hull.

In the morning I brought my mother some toast and water because she had not left her room. I left it at her bedside and said to the shape under the blankets:

There is something for you on the tray. You should take it if you can.

The voice under the blankets said, In a minute.

Minutes later I called from the kitchen table into the house, It'll go cold.

Some words returned along the hall: I'll take it soon.

If I went to two tablets every day, my mother would know she wasn't getting the count wrong. There was only one thing for it, I knew where they were, they were in that blue bag she got at the doctor's on her last visit, the one she put at the back of a different closet in the kitchen. Maybe she thought I didn't see it. Holding a flashlight I rifled a blister pack from the bag and pried it open with my fingernails and in no time at all one of those Xanax, which I called a Double X, was swimming its taste across my tongue before it made the dive down. New pill, but I was used to the general type now. No point in splitting the medication. In less than an hour the thing made it to my head.

That was the end of the dreams of the lights. That's what I said to myself anyway, or was it someone else I said it to, or did someone else say it to me. Anyway.

That same week, one year and one month after my father turned to sticks, by way of a letter totaling seven lines, Pharmalak informed my mother that they were finished with her husband's body.

My mother gazed at the page and repeated some of the words: A burial on Saturday. A car will come.

On that Saturday a limousine did come in the late afternoon, close to sundown. To my left, the moon burned the edge of a snow cloud white to a breezy clear patch in the sky and the lake shone like tinfoil, with the moon so sharp that I could have turned it on its side and cut my finger. My body was wide open because of that tear in the skin and the world rushed in. The car turned right past the gate and onto a small road lined on each side with crosses and headstones until it pulled up to a space in the cemetery where two gravediggers stood with their shovels in front of heaped clay and a ready casket.

We walked up to the graveside. I stared into the hole as a clergyman put his hands on our shoulders:

We should begin, he said.

One of the clouds found the moon and swamped it. A shadow crossed the graveyard, moving across the headstones and reaching us. The diggers and I lifted the coffin, it came up like air, light enough to blow away in a good breeze, inside it some bones and a few heavy things, no doubt, for the illusion. There would not have been much left of him, perhaps a piece of arm, the general shape of a human suggested by the shape of a coffin. Any last-second request to see him would be firmly rejected. The gravediggers handed each other a rope and lowered the casket, put the ropes on the ground and waited. I looked into the hole at my father's remains and wondered what was a father without a body, a collection of places and sounds, what it was we were burying.

What are we burying, I said to her.

The breeze blew at the seconds. Sprinkles wafted down past the high pines of the cemetery.

She was staring at a place far away in the future, or far away in the past, and spoke as if out of this unseen place back to me:

My husband is not dead. I will see him again.

It was the book they gave her, that kind of talk. Magic words that made you see things that weren't there. As for me, I saw a hull instead of a coffin, and water instead of darkness. My father was a sailor underground. Now he could sail it through the clay in the

cemetery. The ship was not the one we made, what floated on the lake the day of the ten tea lights and the rum
aftershave and the announcement of a brother to come.
This ship sailed straight for him the day he was born,
sailed the same distance on calm and windy days. No
weather blew it off course. It sailed for him with an
empty deck, and it arrived for him the moment he died.

The clouds blew away in a breeze and the night
cleared to a patch of stars. I looked into them and
understood how well I was named now. The world was
Sunless inside and out. The man and my mother and
the gravediggers shone in the moon. For a minute I did-
n't know what to think or say, so I thought and said
nothing. The lamps bounced our shadows around the
headstones.

In that coffin lay my father's life with me and mine
with him. Under the ground and under my shoes, he
was oblivious to my mother, to the sky, to the rest of
my life. Maybe we could hold a clinical trial for my
father, find and prosecute the pills in him. The question: Which one of you failed to save him? And one by
one they step forward and give their names, long
names: my name is Atenolol and I failed to save your
father. What this man needed was an operation. More
speak, one hiding behind the other. Yes, we failed in
tandem, though I was the lead medicine and the one
behind me ancillary, to relieve the pain. And
Phenobarbital says, He could have ended it all sooner
if he had taken a certain amount of me, but he did not.

Your father was a strong man. We were there, lying in a bottle, all he had to do was take us out and pour us into his palm and lift his palm and open his mouth and swallow with some water. The inhaler steps forward, still encased in its pumping mechanism, the one that still has some medicine left in it, and it says, Yes, I helped him breathe. I made his suffering last.

We drove away as the diggers crossed the rear-view mirror with their shovels. It was that kind of day when the weather is uncertain, the sky elastic, certain hours can change your life. But I counted nothing of those particular days. They just passed by and went on their way, crossed nameless in their passing, and they may not have recognized me. For the truth was that most days were no different from other days. They had no names. And I was thinner recently.

I slept longer into the next morning of every morning. I counted all the pills in the blue bag: thirty-nine. That was enough for a while if I took one as needed, but what if my mother needed some, what if I needed more. The way to get a script. You tell a story for five minutes and you get it. But I wanted no invention.

The convenience store owner understood why I had to miss days at work and did not mind, he said, as long as I did not make a habit of it. Anyway, I needed the money, since the supply was a concern. One man started to come in regularly when I worked and bought three packs of decongestants—for a bad cold, he said, that wouldn't go away. He sneezed every time when I rang them up on the till. Someone at our school used to talk about decongestants and batteries, a thin fellow from New York with big eyes who didn't come back to school one week and never came back after that week either. This one wasn't buying batteries, but the world is as full of batteries as it is with colds. So the next time I followed him out to the parking lot and asked him if he was buying them in other places too, and what kind of batteries he was using, that I needed to know. I said this in one sentence without even asking his name. We stood in the bare sun and the blustery wind of the desert. He sat on his motorbike and thought a minute with his curly hair and said he would see about my question when he knew who was asking it. I remained friendly to him and did not ask again, kept selling him what he wanted without mentioning that new brand of disease, the eternal cold. The Pakistani remarked on the amount of people buying the medicine, asked me if it was different people, that there was a law about how much you can sell to one person. He asked using hand gestures and I filled in the words. I showed him the names and different driver's license numbers recycled from months back. For my cooperation, in another week I had something new from the decongestant man, something fast for the blood, a small rock of meth. We did the deal in the car outside.

I got Double X's off him too and was able to replace my mother's missing pills, the ones she'd discover were missing when her next count and the days didn't match. Sometimes I forgot to ring up the things he brought to the counter. Sometimes also in the morning someone broke through and asked questions of me about why and to what purpose were all these substances now part of Sunless. I said they lit me up with daylight. If the questions kept coming, going to the closet and opening a pillbox solved that problem, or shaving a thin slice off the rock under hot coffee and drinking the lot. Yes, that sped the problem up and out of my head for a day and more in no time.

I wanted to make my supply last, and while I waited for the questions to go away, the words in my head occasionally had a life of their own because they entered and left of their own accord. The moon lit the whole black world. I sang a song to it one night from my window with a sock on my head to keep it warm: *Salt around me, salt above me. Salt to my right, salt to my left. Look at me now, I'm Doctor Salt.*

My salary at the store did not keep up with the salary of the fellow on the motorbike. I could see he was more a man when he shaved and tidied his appearance a little, maybe thirty-five, and his language changed now that the two of us were made of business. He said he understood about the money, that there could be credit but also interest. Stuff on credit was a loan. Same principle, he said.

My mother, meanwhile, was often gone from the house, she spent more time downtown at the temple. One day I noticed she was taking more of the pills, there was a broken one in the pillbox in the counter, mixed well down into it as if she needed to hide from herself what she was doing. She was taking another half on top of the one, and around the box in the closet were crayons from when I was young, she must have put them there. I smelled a child in them, smelled the shapes I made, the bird I drew with the explanations. I smelled the baby's crib I lay in, the warm paste of food she fed me from a spoon.

After work a couple of days later my mother got up late and appeared behind me, moving smartly to the stove where she put a kettle on with water and tore two pieces of bread out of the plastic for toast.

How are you, she said.

I'm fine.

She was moving quicker than I'd seen her move in years. I could have been the boy in the garden again, she could have been the woman in the windows, and we were waving to each other in and out of the sunlight. This image stayed a moment and was replaced with us standing dimly in the dark kitchen. I had hung a crimson sheet over the window with a nail sometime recently, some sun leaked in along the rip and made it to the floor before it withered.

I was thinking, she said, shaking her dressing gown free of the wrinkles that had grown into it, about Mr. Swan next door. Have you seen him?

No. I never see him.

Can you look out for him for me?

I walked to the kitchen window and pulled the sheet to the left. I could see only the front garden of Swan's house, and he wasn't in it, never was, the long grass went in every direction but up.

When I came home from work the next day I knocked on his door, the television was loud enough, the flash of it through the blinds. I went inside to where he was sitting in the armchair with a cane. Swan fought in an old war and now wore a blue baseball cap with the gold name of a navy ship on it I never heard of. He watched black-and-white films of planes with trails of smoke streaming out of them screaming down into ships and exploding. His face was a white prune dangling to a mouth that leaked. The screen he was watching had divided itself into two and sent both parts, one into each eye, where they flashed at the same time. An orange flash, the sound of a gun.

Mr. Swan, I said. Can I get you anything?

A Cookie, he said, I'd love one.

He turned half way to the back, and I went to the kitchen and found the cookies and made him tea. They were the two things he had plenty of, tea and cookies, the diet of Mr. Swan. I sat beside him and he did not move, did not react as we watched the old war, the guns pound at the air, splashing smoke in fists around the dots of diving planes. It was good to be in his company. The history in him didn't talk.

A break came and the program went to a Newsflash. A voice spoke over the image of a man looking horrified at a television:

The government today raised the terror alert from yellow to orange based on raw intelligence of a possible attack within the next three months on an unidentified city on the east coast. And now this: Do you fear a sudden, unjustified assault in your house by a casual friend, or even a family member? Discussing politics one minute, trading blows the next? Researchers warn that fear of terrorism is raising anxiety levels nationwide. Persistent Threat Syndrome, or PTS, is a serious medical condition. Talk to your doctor. Elevax: the alternative medicine for anxiety. Now for a weather update, we go to Mike in downtown Salt Lake City. Mike, what's the weather doing tonight?

That must have been the news, I thought. I hadn't watched television in a long time, but I must have said it out loud because next thing the old fellow next to me moved his head:

They're selling fear.

What?

He turned to me with the plate of cookies. You should really try one of these.

I left and told my mother that he was fine, eating and relaxing in his armchair. Meanwhile the interest I was paying to motorcycle man overtook the principle. There were strong words in the parking lot outside the store, talk of collection, another word I knew from the bank demands on the phone. He arrived with two older men on motorcycles.

So it happened that some of the houses around ours began to empty of certain goods. Then the threats went away. I went back to Mr. Swan and took the television when he was asleep on the armchair. I unplugged it and carried it out, a very good television with features he never used anyway, bought by relatives, a sister in another state: he had told someone he would like a television, and that person told someone about getting him one. Well she could buy him another one to replace it. And not having his television didn't stop Swan watching it. I saw him in his armchair the next day through a fold in the blinds, looking at where it was missing.

The problem of supply and demand. Downtown I read the backs of the free newspapers for drug trials, running a finger down the advertisements for symptoms, syndromes, studies, the lists. In the Salt Lake City area I found two clinical trials, Restless Leg Syndrome and Generalized Anxiety Disorder, both conducted at Pharmalak. I called the number and gave a woman my details, which were mostly correct.

Now that things were better between me and the decongestant motorcyclists, I built up an excellent supply. I had no reason to raid my mother's stuff in the kitchen but kept an eye on how much she used. She was definitely moving about the house faster and even went out to the back yard and spread seed for birds again, talked about us going into town and seeing a film one night, wouldn't that be nice, she wanted to know. At first I thought it was the temple people straightening her out. She wore perfume again, a ghost's art, just enough, I no longer smelled it when she was out of the room. She seemed a bit more like a real person, whatever that was, her lively stare, and layered above that, her black hair, and another layer, this time her face, painted over her body and set in place. The problem was that I was a little out of myself, and when her mouth moved to speak, another layer floated about her, this time of sound and words that didn't match up fully, and I knew it was all fakery: if we touched accidentally my hand would go through her, or she would shimmer once and dissolve in ripples. One of us was a lie.

So she was the lie.

I was suspicious. Why all this sudden interest in me, in anything. And suddenly the old red dress was out of her closet. There was only one explanation for this attitude and this behavior: she was taking something that didn't belong to her. She found the meth, the other assortment of amphetamines that I recently purchased with my injection of cash, and she was secreting those substances into herself. I hadn't counted them recently.

When she mentioned the film again that afternoon, I asked her had she been in my room. I had no proof but thought I might bluff it. We were standing in the kitchen. I kept an eye on where she might glance in answer to my questions.

I said, Have you been in my room?

Not since your father died.

Did you go in by accident? I said. I mean by that more recently.

She still said no by shaking her head and walked right up to me until I smelled her shampoo.

She said, I'd like us to be friends, go out together more.

There was no denying it, this way of a real person about her, the eyes wider, her hair combed, her eyes clear. But I looked at her and all I could see was a certain number of tablets missing in my room. My blood ran with suspicion. To be like this she must have entered my room and took them, no other explanation. I thought she was on the slow pills. She was on the fast pills. And they were mine. Slow woman turns into fast woman. That explained the half tablet in the slow pills. She must have been taking a half less than before, not a half more, weaning herself off them. Was there a different explanation? She wanted to be a fast woman.

She smiled and held out her arms and I watched the hands at the ends of them, and she said *Jimmy* and stepped forward and moved them around and up my back.

I'm so sorry for all the years I've been sad, she said. I missed your brother, more than I should have, I never held him, I woke and he was gone.

She squeezed me tighter. I felt a woman where my mother had been. This was wrong.

She said, We can go back to Chicago, we can leave this place.

I leaned into her and held her too, counting what I had hidden in my mattress. I would have to do a count. The cost to me of this affection. I needed a padlock for my door. The betrayal of her own son just to be a different woman.

What about Chicago? I said.

We can go back to Chicago, your father and I were happy there. You can be too.

No, I said. I'm staying here. But you go if you want.

The words came first and then I did the tiny lean for her to move back: You don't have any money to move, I said. We go from month to month with the bills as it is.

She shrank to some pleading words. The bills will come no matter where we live. Your father would have wanted it.

I can't, I have to stay here, I said, and left her standing with herself in the kitchen. The next day I locked my bedroom door using a padlock looped through a hole in a steel plate I'd screwed into the door frame.

I was thinner, more bone in me, the way my father had gone before me. That saying about the apple always falling close to the tree. I would have to buy new clothes.

Some more things emptied out of houses nearby and I had new clothes.

What happened now was that I had so much stored up, including some goods I kept stacked up the walls in my room I hadn't sold yet, a brass Empire turntable, vinyl records from a collector, a laptop, so many odds and valuables, that I wondered if I needed to keep working at all. Some of the clothes I nailed to the windows of the whole house. One day the store owner repeated a count of things on the shelves, so from then I met the motorcycles out of town along the highway until I stopped going to work. That is what transpired because the phone rang and the store owner left a message, the man from Pakistan with the verbs and nouns crammed into his talk: You steal. I have receipts. I count.

My mother was listening behind my back, What is he saying? She searched my eyes. I noticed a little of the speed moving out of her. She must have run out of the fast pills because she couldn't break into my room to steal them. The padlock was doing its work. She looked panicked, restless with her hands, breathing funny, slipping back down into the land of down and dead. Not my problem, not my head. The tablets that fueled her new life did not fall free out of the trees. An hour later I left a half a slice on the counter, a portion to sacrifice for proof, a necessary sacrifice, and went for a walk around the block.

Some hand snatched it from the altar, because it wasn't there when I got back. And she was gone from the house: I looked for her, she had disappeared. I went into my room past definite evidence that the padlock had been worked at with a screwdriver—those gouges in the door frame. Inside the room I checked the mattress at once. I separated it at the right place: yes, still there, those lovely little moons and suns, Double X's, amphetamine allsorts, the meth. I made the water boil in the kettle on the bedroom table, dropped into a mug the last slice off the rock that was now a big grain and dissolved it in hot coffee, stirred it well in, drank it. Waited. Not so long, not too long.

The surge of the bed falling up, the white sheet fabric colliding big with me, everything.

I drank some water to wash down a yellow pill, watched television into the evening. She did not come home. The box droned from the living room, a forecast for the first winter storm, winds from the north. I lit a fire and the flames sparked over the wood. In my bedroom I watched as the lake drained the day out of the sky, watched the salt bed for lights; but nothing moved out there in miles of ghost white that shone like a weak battery into the rest of the universe.

At some time, I think a long time into the night, I thought I heard her door close. She was back: I knocked on her bedroom door.

Yes? The voice was hers. Stronger, clearer—just the one word told me that. I went inside. She was lying in the bed with that book on her chest.

She said, I don't need those pills anymore. I'm off them. I know how to do it without medicine, without symptoms.

She closed her eyes. She was shaking and her face was white and gray at the same time. The temple people must have told her she could stop taking the amphetamines, the pram pills, to read the book.

I stepped out of her room and made for the mattress in mine, stuffing everything into a bag except for a few days' supply. I combed my hair and dressed in a large raincoat, then a smaller one on top of that, and set out left along the street. The wide concrete street had some cracks in it where grass grew in clumps, the street white and blowing with salt. I saw my hand bigger than ever floating in front of me somewhere attached to the rest of me and to the bag as I crossed the highway, made for the lake, breathing deep, breathing all the salt I could. There was a new pain in my head and a dry tongue that the walk did not take away. I would bury those pills to hide them from my mother. I must have walked a while because the sky moved with me, wheeling new stars out until I reached the place where we had played those years ago. Antelope Island rose ahead, a blank triangle cut out of stars. The salt gleamed at the shore like ice. I took my shoes and socks off and waded out into the cold water with the chill draping my ankles. In a Salt Lake

City winter the moon lowers a white straw and sucks every ounce of heat off the face of the world. The sky wheeled out that moon, rolling it thin on the edge, a slice of it fell off and drifted on the water. I felt heat rise off my body like steam and the cold climb into my bones to replace it. And just as swiftly, the pills took the cold and lifted it a little out of me, and I was above and bright like a sun, I was everything, I was beyond hot and cold.

I dug into the salt, down a foot, and placed the bag in there and scooped back the salt above it, smoothing the surface. I walked a few yards and turned around, looked at the burial site and saw no trace of the burial.

Think. The last time here. With my parents, when my brother was on his way, the four of us splashing around in a warm blue lake of summer. Now my father was dead, so that was three left, and my brother never lived at all, which meant we were down to two; but I was not here either—all the lights were off in the world and I was walking in black, and except for the cold in my feet, I had no evidence of being alive myself and could never prove it to anyone. I walked into the waves and put my head under the water into a different night and waited until it sliced at my lips and forehead before cutting its ice down my neck and shoulders. I had not taken enough, it was not lasting. I opened my eyes in the shock, all black, brushstrokes of black water, starless black beating of a heart in my ears. My heart, it must have been. My eyes were slits. Under the water, I looked around. And above me I saw a white pill move along the surface, dissolving in waves.

Into the black I said, I need a brother in this life. Come back to me.

Sooner or later I was going to run out. I was already running low, enough for a month, and when my mother's bottles went empty with no sign of her going to the doctor? What then? I could not go back to work, and she had the rest of the life insurance money in a bank, I could not get to it. It was best to go with the motorcycle crowd with the permanent colds: they lived out near the border with Nevada, the straight road west through the salt flats. I called a number, told them I was coming, that I would be on the highway. In the house I left three days' supply of fast pills in a bag tied to the padlock. After those few days she would have to find her own while I was gone. She should have stayed on the sad pills, what she could get legally and plenty of them too.

I made a mask of her red dress, scissor-holes for eyes, drove out to the convenience store with the wind rifling the contents of the back seat asking me, What did you steal. The owner, the face of him behind the register. I walked with the apron on and he pretended to reach down for a gun where there was no gun. He ran around at me, shouting for me to get out. I have gun. I shoot gun. I had the dress arranged in a lofty manner about my head, a bow-tie of arms on top. His fat legs filled the aisle with a stumpy run and I blessed him with two throws of peppered water, through the holes of my mask

I watched him stoop and grab at his eyes and shout.

From the store I took the cold medicine, paint, lighter fluid, batteries, drain cleaner, camping fuel, and Windex. That left the ammonia and some other things for later, the basic list was for me to gather. I threw them into the back seat for the wind to find and drove left and west out of the lot. Soon enough up behind me they came, the motorcycles, one with a girl, she smiled at me, the sound of one engine in the four bikes. They surged ahead and I followed them on the highway till we passed the speedway on the right. They tilted into a road that led to a two-storey house at the end of a large yard, a high wall behind it. In after them I went, floating fast. We ran through the rotted doors into rooms of stripped windows with bed sheets hung off nails. We slid couches off to the walls, tore up the carpet to some wood and holes. From the corners dust ran across the air with its hands up. They had two labs in two bathrooms, in the tubs. I walked past an open door, the girl hitched her skirt up and sat on the battery man, he ran his hands under her shirt, then tight at her neck, then down to where she was bare underneath. She sat harder, tightened her legs to the thigh bones and closed her eyes. He knelt behind her and pulled up the skirt and slapped her. I lifted the bottle of whiskey to make the pills flat across me just under the skin. I had taken the biggest dose yet and it was too sharp: I floated ahead of myself, bumping into things.

In the evening the battery man brought me into one

bathroom and said, Here is the recipe for crystal meth. Now pay attention. He pointed to his temple. No notes—all up here.

He was a professor somewhere for a while in another state and his breath stank. I knew that last detail every time I met him at the store. He crushed the cold medicine in with some gasoline and heated them until the Psuedophedrene distilled, then combined some lithium with a little ammonia and produced Red Phosphorus. He added iodine to it and then mixed everything in with the Psuedophedrene and said to let it heat. He brought me to the other bathroom where the same mix had heated for two days. On it he poured some drain cleaner, the sodium hydroxide, he said, and added the lighter fuel as solvent. I saw the two fluids separate: on one side the dark, and on the other side the clear.

The dark is the waste, he said. The clear is the meth.

He waved a ruler above them as they parted, and singing mixed the battery acid with rock salt, the Hydrogen Chloride gas, he said, and injected it into the clear fluid, which fizzed up.

I name you Crystal Meth, he said above the sink.

All those scientific names for what you get in a store. For months I lorded over this mix, separated only by aisles and prices, and I never knew.

We melted into our own rooms, it was a big house once—for a family no doubt. The girl with him was pretty, for that reason I did not see how tall she was or not tall, her dress, her name: all those ingredients burned away to the pretty in her. She walked by my room a couple of times, then twice more, the fifth time she hung there like a painting, the necklace string on her neck.

Well, she said.

I lay on sacks and coats, the walls were black. Her lips moved at mine. She said, My dad would like you. I'm going to stop soon.

I asked her if the fellow in the next room was her boyfriend.

She said he was her teacher at college before she dropped out. He trusts me now. He brings me to the salt to bury the stuff.

I asked her what bury in the salt meant.

She sat on the bed, a finger with a broken nail to her lips. I saw that she was naked, now that she was so close in the dark.

She said, After midnight some nights we take the motorcycles across the lake bed and hide it in the salt in transparent bags. He says it's the perfect place to make the crystals invisible.

So that was the lights, I said.

What?

She had a small notebook in her hands. What's this on the bed?

I thought I must have wanted to read something or write something because the pencil was in my right hand. There it is, I said, lifting the pencil, and we both laughed.

She giggled. I like this notebook. Can I have it?

I did not want to say no, so I said, My father gave it to me when I was young.

Then you shouldn't be leaving it lying around, She smiled at me again. I'm going to stop soon.

She stood and the sacks on the bed barely moved, she was thin, she walked her weak pink under the door frame and went right in the black hall on the broken boards to the room to my right. I heard the man's gentle words to her through the wall, I heard her sigh presently, I shone a light onto the pages of the notebook, the pencil and the child's drawings, the blue bird, what my mind and memory put there with the pencil. I closed the pages and the book disappeared, as black as the walls.

The sun spun for ten days, we made meth and were merry, and on the fifteenth day battery man went to the shed and drove out his antique black Volkswagen Beetle. He waited while the four of us got in and drove out in his black coat with a high collar and gloves with the headlights turned off until we were chugging silent smoke along the houses of the town, and then he selected one particular road, and another one to the end of a cul-de-sac.

The owners are out for the evening, he said.

We had until midnight, and with the headlights turned off he drove the car past the high hedges and up a winding private road and sidled to the side of this big house. The engine stopped in the black night. A cat ran off the mat under the porch light. Someone said we shouldn't chance it, the police, and he turned and asked them to say that again, that this was his gift to us, this place of refuge, he said, signaling to the window. All this I give you.

He let us out and drove behind the house and came back with a large key he stuck into the door.

Such a big house. The long hall with carpets, the tiled kitchen, the dining room with an oak table, the living room with a fireplace and tongs and paintings of the sea and men with gray wet umbrellas, the master bedroom and the big bed. We lit candles and used them as torches leading our faces hither and thither.

Light a fire, battery man said, and a fire was lit, the wood stacked already, a candle was dipped to it.

Now let us be free, he said, and strip ourselves of the twenty-first century.

Everyone stripped and followed him as he ran from room to room with an open book before him and the candle in another hand. The existentialist room, he said. Strip the room! And we took the paintings off the wall and stacked the chairs and piled everything in one heap, whatever was loose in the house.

All is stripped to what we can see, he said. They surround themselves with walls and call it home, this illusion, and they take it into themselves. Don't you see? Can't you see? These bastards. All my life I've had to deal with this. They don't want my ideas to be heard, you mark my words.

And I saw that he was screaming, his veins were lit.

I drifted back to the kitchen, heard the whooping from a distant room. The kitchen was dark and silent. My candle lit the sink and part of the faucet that dripped every five seconds. An invisible tiny mouse struggled for twenty minutes to pull the blue stick of poison through the tiny crack and into the channels under the floor. I imagined the busy mouth attached at the other side, the effort to get its death into a small hole and down to where it could hide it and know it was there and go back and have a feast. I put my fingers around the stick to pinch it out and away, and the mouse went still. I could not get my fingers around it. A while later the rustling came back and the stick was gone. The suicide of a mouse.

Down the hall she came, pink out of the shadows.

There you are, she said. He was asking about you. I said I'd find you.

I asked her what his name was.

She said in a whisper, His name is de Cherchy, that's what he wants to be called.

Her voice went back up: He got fired from his philosophy job at the university because they couldn't handle who he was. He's going to be famous one day. He's writing a book of philosophy that will really shake things up, so big he won't show me. That's why he can't touch this stuff, he has to stay on whiskey for the concentration. I dropped out when he got fired. I don't need a piece of paper to tell me who I am. She placed one arm on each side of my neck and kissed my forehead, her lips were soft and dry at the same time.

I'm eighteen now, she said.

I broke a crystal and we shared it in the candlelight, her tongue out and I placed it softly upon her tongue, she wiggled it and laughed, I sagged and sighed in fast dreams, we danced to the music of the spheres the professor said were ringing in the universe. We were mice, we scampered room to room, we flowed over furniture, we dove together into the carpet and rolled around as de Cherchy read from the book and a bottle. The basic principle of philosophy, he said, is what do we know. Where is the form, find the form. We ran the tiled kitchen, we ran the rugged halls, we heard him calling to us.

Then we drifted to different rooms. In the living room the fire was blazing high in the hearth. I saw de Cherchy spread naked from the armchair to his sandals, lounging in green velvet armchair edged with gold braid. His hairy belly bulging into a scratch, his beard moved as he spoke down to the girl sitting at his feet.

I remained silent at the door. I was cold in the kitchen. I liked the heat of this fire.

He talked softly to her, The ghost that you call forth, you'll never be rid of it. That's the truth. The meth is in you and it repeats. You are never cured.

He joined his hands. But you don't want a cure. The best medicine is to take what you don't need. That's the power of choice.

The girl drew circles in the carpet with her finger. He splashed an inch of whiskey onto his face and went on:

With choice, you can say, I'm not afraid. He tapped his chest. You say, Wait a second, I am my own person. They've had control of me my whole life, and now I have to go to college? He parted and made his hands flow left and right, What, do I have to study this and this? The choice says, No. The choice says, Hey, you need to know that I am, to begin with—I am. He held up a finger. And I am not, that's the second thing they need to hear. I am not going to, you know.

Shhhh, the girl said. You're tired.

She rubbed de Cherchy's leg and leaned her head against the shin.

I wish I knew what you know, she said. She was crying. You will. Come here.

He saw the glint on her neck and traced a necklace in his hands to a gold cameo. He opened it.

What's this?

My parents, she said.

Family, he said.

He left it in his open palm and watched the flames until she crawled to them and threw it. He smiled and stroked her hair and placed his hands around her face when she moved to his lap.

Her mouth sought his and they kissed, and she traced the kiss down his stomach, to his wide and spread thighs, moved her tongue up between them and closed her mouth over him and sank down.

Rachel, he said. No one knows who you really are. You have destroyed your ties for me.

The fire caught fire in his eyes. He moved behind her, moved himself on top of her, she was a skeleton with skin, she was tiny under him, her face straining for pleasure.

I shrank back to the cold kitchen, and the house became silent. So her name was Rachel. I had not asked her name.

In a while I saw him leave the living room with the shadows clinging to him before they let go and he sat himself at the kitchen table and unscrewed the whiskey bottle and sipped, looked carefully at me.

There are viruses, he said, out there. And they watch us.

I looked out the black window. Where are they.

Have one hope, he said, that a virus never knows itself. I am writing about this, what is in preparation, my book that the publishers refuse to print for fear of these ideas.

What virus, I said.

He said, Do you know that scientists found decay from *mycobacterium tuberculosis,* the disease that killed them, in the spines of Egyptian mummies after four thousand years?

He leaned into the candle: Since the beginning of the Christian calendar, only forty-six generations have lived, the life of an average person multiplied by forty-six. The truth is, we differ little from our ancestors.

He made a sound of a deck of cards flipping under a thumb.

But parasites can go through 2,000 generations in a month, or 180,000 years in human life, they speed through life and death so fast (de Cherchy threw up his hands) that we can see them evolve before our eyes. Dying means perfection to them. So pray that a virus never develops knowledge of itself, never sees itself reflected on a river surface and asks any one of three terrible questions.

What three questions, I said.

He made a fist and opened one finger at a time: Who am I. What do I want. Who has what I want.

So who has what you want, I said.

He laughed. Smart man. Leave her alone. That's what I want.

I said, I have.

You didn't. You allowed *her* not to leave *you* alone. It took me a long time to develop her. Those poems, her thoughts, what I had to listen to when she was a student and now here. I will send you away with nothing. You'll go back with nothing.

The candle blew with the breath of nothing, fluttered with the word.

Good, I thought, he was battery man again, too much of de Cherchy.

At his word, within the hour, the group gathered ourselves and went out to the Beetle and eased down the winding road and turned into speed on the highway. It seemed longer than six hours since we came, a trace of light was in the low sky, some birds sang out of branches.

I wondered why the owners had not come back, why the cat was waiting at the door when we came first, a cat knows when the owners are in the house.

We reached the building of the methalated bathrooms and moved silently to our rooms and lay on the beds. The following afternoon, battery man came out to where I stood at the end of the roadway facing the main road, stood beside me and brushed his curly hair back and sighed.

What way is it then between you and her, he said.

He walked a step to my right. I saw the black handle of a pistol.

I said nothing. I had just taken a pocketful of crystals, what I found in the bathroom. I had no money and he had offered nothing for these two weeks or more of work, the complete process of making meth I had done many times since the first time, and on my own. That should have earned me something. But I think I was supposed to beg, this was the program, I was to beg and he would loan it to me and I would work it off with interest. I had enough of his mouth and I was not going to ask for anything.

He must have been watching as I took the stuff or had his own cameras and caught me going to my car because here we both were, standing on the main road by the open door of my car. I had been relieving myself of the water I drank and out he comes to me, quiet, but I heard him alright. He held a scanner in his left hand, his right hand on that small gun or whatever it was in there.

I said, Don't worry, there's nothing between me and her.

There was plenty between him and her, enough to make him close the distance to me completely.

He said, I'm not worried. Three questions: Did you take anything out of the bathroom? Do you still have what you took? Is it in your pocket?

His hand was at my pocket and his fingers were shoved in and twirling inside for the crystals I stole. I could not let him hand all that pain into my future by taking them from me now.

We moved together in a dance, arm in arm for the right tilt, but he was a different weight and out of breath. I lifted a rusted exhaust pipe I saw on the ground with the jags at the end of it and stuck him in the lip and sliced out part of his gum, a tooth came out as well, he shook like a child in awe of a toy, the scream like a word he was practicing, so it was just the high and such a very long breath. The cruel ones are always surprised at how much pain hurts.

With the same pipe I banged him on the head, flat on top, both his eyes swiveled loose up and drew themselves to the bang. I dragged him well off the road, gouged out a hole silently in the salt and put him in it, tied his hands with his own pants and asked if he was okay now, saw him plead with his eyes curled up to his own head for the bit of light remaining. When I filled everything in, the salt bulged and fell at his mouth and I patted it. He woke I suppose, screamed somehow once through the salt. That's ridiculous, I said, a wrong and unnatural act to breathe in salt like that, I would take dying before that. I waited until the heaving stopped, and I drove off.

He was the leader and the rest were followers. What happens to followers when the leader is not to be found.

On the way I dragged on a cigarette with the distant pills at home in the fridge pleading for me to find them, they were swaying in a kind of song, though I wasn't worried now, I had my independence now. I saw in the rear-view mirror the ground heave, not possible, heard the man I buried call to me from under the salt. Not possible. Shut up, I said. Shut up for a second, I'm trying to think.

He went quiet in the grave, or else I was too far away to hear the heaving. I cleaved the desert with the steady hum of the car. It was a breezy day where the wind seemed to blow the sun across the sky a bit quicker to get it to the other side.

At my mother's house I found three fat newspapers in plastic tubes. I opened the door to the hallway, poured a bath, soaked in the hot water. Then I thought it would be nice to make the place clean for her, so I swept and washed the floors, opened the windows within reason, washed the dishes. I had it in my mind to clean, and for a few minutes or hours I washed the walls with bleach and soap, spreading thick swaps with a sponge. I lay in bed and let the open windows blow the smell of salt around the room. The salt made the second part of the day whiter, and the blue of the sky at the top of the window tinged the walls, and then the blue and the white and the smell scurried around the floor, blown around by the breeze across the lake, the great shallow lake, the lake that lived inside a great desert. I had been awake all the night before, but that meant nothing at this point. I had my bottle of water, my lake.

Later when I reached inside my pocket I found nothing: battery man had somehow grabbed the entire handful and held onto them even in the fight, and I had buried them clutched in his fist. Or they lay invisible across the salt, lost treasure. His last act, to grab and not let go, what he did in life he does in leaving it. The addiction is both ways, has two faces, taker and giver. This was the panic in my thinking then, that I must drive out to that house again and dig him up out of the ground.

On the bedroom door hung the padlock minus the bag with the three days' supply of fast pills. So she had taken them. In the days since then she must have recovered with the help of her book, or else found more speed if the book's chemistry did not set her blood racing with something else.

The chemistry in me was different, it was the particular mix of that most recent batch in the manufacturing house. I was unsteady, I could not stop surging, perhaps it was a stronger mix and it needed to be diluted somehow. Half a day later already, and no sign of an end to the surge: my body was a light, there was no dark in me, and I was without a problem in the world except how to keep it lit. Where was my mother? What was wrong with me. Something was wrong with me.

In the kitchen I took her pillboxes from the closet and emptied the slow tablets onto the table. She must have been to the doctor again. I watched carefully as they rolled across the polished surface. I leaned down to smell the wood polish, the lemon brand she liked to use, saw where she rubbed, the swirls and circles when she polished the wood, must have been when she was living fast for that while. I folded a cloth and rubbed it anti-clockwise to play her back to me, to see if I could hear what she was thinking when she polished.

I saw how the tablets had rolled into shapes and studied them for an omen and then looked at the leaflet that came with the medicine: effects, side effects, precautions, antidotes, drawings of chemical properties, and near the top, in big type, Lorazepam. I was a young boy again, I reached out my arm and swept the table and watched the pills sail across the kitchen and hit the opposite wall. They fell even though they tried to use their wings to stay in the air, they scattered across the floor, the things that stole my mother.

I stepped on one just to hear it die. What a thing that is, to randomly kill a pill.

In the corners and between the tiles on the floor they seemed to taunt me until I picked them up and counted them back into one tight pillbox and put them into the fridge, where they sang to me like sirens. We know you want us, Sunless, we know you want us. In a pile they sang their anthem. We are the few now. We are the only few.

Only if you get a hold of me, I said.

I imagined tying myself to a chair. I went to the chair, sat down, heard the creak. I stood, felt the slots where my arms might be tied to stop me putting those voices into me. No, I grabbed the chair, lifted it, felt its small weight. It had no voice, nothing to say to me at all, even though it must have known what I was about to do. I threw it across the room. I opened the fridge and took them out again and counted them all in case a couple had run off or were hiding. There's always one. I swept up the remains of the dead one and poured it back. I lined up my mother's Lori's Prams and introduced myself, told them this was a new situation and we all had to get used to it.

I have duties for each of you, so line up in formation. You, what do you do? And you?

I don't know, the pill says, I do the same as all the others.

A different one nods to the one beside it, Same as him.

Another says, It doesn't matter what has happened to you.

What do you mean, I said.

It says, You are what you take for what you are.

I agreed and slipped it into my mouth when it finished speaking, I was sailing closer to the sirens. The pills did not have a lot of room in my head to bother me because of the questions already crowding my head. I needed to ask the pills those questions about my mother, what the relationship between them and my mother was, how well they knew her now after so many years.

I wrote my name on the table using the pills, it was S-U-N-L-E-S-S, they spelled the word without comment. I reached to the sides and shook the table and the word rocked off into circles, the letters shook my name away. A history of the chemical: first pills, then a name, and unto pills they did return.

A voice sounded behind me, out in the hall.

Sunless?

I had not spoken. It was not my mother's voice. The voice came from down the hall, from the other side of the door, out on the street.

I said, Who is that?

The slot for the letters in the front door at the end of the hall opened, I knew the sound of that slot.

Is that you, the voice said. Did you spell your name just now? Is that your real name?

I said nothing, bent to the level of the sound, saw a

mouth move again in the slot. Words like whispers, a breeze around the house: Where is your father?

I checked the doors and windows, all closed and shut of sunlight, but still someone standing at the slot in the door or riding in on top of the whispers, like the voice of my father's cigarettes. Whispers floated into the kitchen, and on top of the whispers, or inside them, I heard more words:

Where is your mother?

I said, I don't know.

Where is your father?

Just one second, I said

I ran for the door and yanked it open, felt the wind of huge wings evaporating. I rushed to the gate, nothing on either side all the way down the pavement. Two white shirts in an open window down the street, must have just been the breeze on them flapping. I checked the letterbox, it was stuffed with new mail, bank mail, final demands in red. I ran hands down my body and felt a chest, hips, a thigh. I switched on the light because it was dark outside. Yes, I could see myself clearly. It was me.

Standing at the front door I called my mother's name back into the house: Are you there?

An answer came down the hall, my last word bouncing back to me. I went to her door, knocked three times and slowly.

No answer.

She went back to Chicago without me. Or she disappeared, got that disease.

I went into the room, the bed was unmade and her slippers waited on the floor.

Maybe tomorrow morning I would wake and find her lying in bed or in the kitchen, returned from her downtown friends. Maybe we decide to plan for the rest of our lives, new lives, films, trips, she tells me about how she grew up, about her parents, things we'd never talked about before. We laugh, she strokes my hair, and I go out and get a job and find friends and live a normal life. That was the plan if I found her or she found me. We could be together now that I was on the sad pills too, they would marry us mother and son.

I was still in her room when I heard the voice again calling. Keep talking, I said to myself and rummaged through the sheets, lifted the carpet, checked behind the door. Keep talking and I'll follow your voice and find you. I traced the voice to the pillbox in the kitchen closet and emptied them out and I ate the one that seemed to be calling me, it went quiet after I swallowed it. No, it didn't have a whole lot to say then. My stomach very briefly floated off and I had to run after it to get it back.

The television was flashing, Swan's television in the living room. I placed my arms flat on the sides of the armchair, long fat strings of blood. I listened to the blood. I looked inside my arm and followed a blood vessel to the heart, swam the pipes into and out of the chambers of my heart. In there, squeezed together, was everything I remembered and everything I couldn't forget. They were in the same chambers and wanted to be the same things, but they weren't exactly the same things. What I couldn't forget was stronger. From the fabric of my father's armchair rose the smell of the cigarettes he smoked into the evening.

What my father had breathed out over a year ago, I breathed in, a last breath from his lungs into mine, delayed a year. The clock circled to nine o'clock.

I sat in the dark stabbed at with the television light and watched breaking news, two jets roaring off an aircraft carrier. I thought it was news, but the camera pulled back and showed a concerned family huddled to their television, watching the jets. It was about people watching the news. While I watched, a voice spoke as the fighters soared toward the top of the stolen television:

Feel secure again. Remember that person? Talk to your family about your values. Talk to your doctor about Elevax.

Predictably I heard the pills shouting in the kitchen, I took another one to shut them up and washed it down with water and put the rest of them in a plastic bag and zipped it shut and put it into the freezer.

Shout all you want now, I said.

I was so tired I wondered if this was what being dead was, what being dead for a day was like. I read once that a good way to live was to act as if you were already dead. So a plan came to me: buy a coffin or bang one together with wood and nails, sleep in it for a night and take note of what I could not change now that I was dead. When I wake I will remember what I wanted to do.

The evidence was that she had left, but she might not be gone at all. I wondered if it was possible to live in a house with another person and never see each other. One leaves for work, the other arrives home, they miss each other. Messages on the telephone, notes on the table, food eaten from the fridge, living with someone and never seeing them for days and weeks. I came up with a strategy: to stretch my arms to the walls while I walked along corridors, to brush against her if she passed.

When my mother and I did meet, would I even recognize her? We'd never been apart for this long, and so I never committed her face to memory. There must have been times when I talked to her without looking, listened to her without looking, handed her letters or breakfast without looking, said goodbye without looking. I never snapped pictures. Now that she was missing, I could not be sure what she really looked like, and the trouble was that if I went to the police station to enquire after her, they might ask me for a description. I should find photographs of her and check the faces I met against them. What if the police said they needed to know what my mother sounded like.

The sound of my mother's voice, I'd heard it from birth, but I didn't have a recording. I could recover how she spoke by repeating words she said often, this word soft, that word loud, or find a shopping list she wrote and imagine the hand that wrote it. I practiced speaking in her voice: Sunless, can you talk a little more, just for me? Yes, I could put the parts together and hear her voice again. But one truth was evident: the sound of her voice was nowhere in this house.

In the kitchen closet I found two photographs in the bag she brought from the hospital when she went to have my brother. In one she looked fifteen years old, long hair, she sat in the middle of other boys and girls in a meadow. In the other she was maybe twenty, she lay at a river's edge with a couple of girls and some young men dressed in neat shirts and white pants. I found too in that blue bag the following: a plastic brown wallet, an envelope with a lock of my hair on my first birthday, a picture of her own mother.

I had to fix the two raincoats so they fit better, because they were drying and getting tighter on me, especially the smaller one on the outside. In the living room I finally pulled them off my body and flapped them while bending forward as I watched the news.

Running under the headline *Outrage!* the screen showed silent security camera film of a broad-shouldered and hooded man slapping a frail woman's head in the dim foyer of an apartment block. She swayed at the first blow. At the second she crumbled around her walking stick and fell out of the film. The man bent and rummaged at her, then he stood and put something in the pocket of his padded coat. He said something, wagged a finger down to her, and walked out to the street. For thirty seconds the film showed the woman's legs lying still. Then they moved. Then the woman's head.

A banner flashed: *102-Year Old Woman Beaten and Robbed.*

Police are asking for the public's assistance in tracking down this man, the newsreader said, as a still of the robber's head expanded to fit the whole screen. She turned to the other newsreader.

We've been running this segment for three days—and what an enormous outpouring of support for that unfortunate woman!

The other newsreader nodded and turned to the camera: And now this message.

The commercial showed two short videos and a photo in turn. In the first, soldiers missing one or both legs wavered between two railings on their new prosthetics in a hospital. In the second, emaciated teenagers spurning food under the gaze of anxious parents at a table. Last, a black-and-white photo of women and men sitting in the lounge of a retirement home, staring into the flash of the lens with their shrunken backs and bloated legs.

When the sound returned, a man wearing glasses in a white coat sat at a desk staring at the camera, as if the viewer was sitting on the other side of his desk:

Are you experiencing Body Image Distortion? Are you lonely? Can't leave the house due to age or disability? Do you view yourself differently from how others see you, and you just can't face any more scrutiny of your physical appearance? BID is a serious medical condition. But help is on the way. Call Pharmalak for information on an imminent medical treatment for Body Image Distortion.

I went to the bathroom and saw my face, felt it with my fingers, saw the light beard. Last time I looked in the mirror there was none. Good thing I didn't have to go to work in the store today. I held a new razor blade and dragged it across my right cheek and felt the tug of the whiskers back until a few snapped away. To make it easier I rubbed soap in my hands and added water until it foamed a little and then spread it across the hairs. The mirror steamed a little with the hot water, the beard disappeared in strips as I dragged the blade over my face.

No doubt about it—the house had got thinner while I was away. My mother must have sold the mandolin, the cabinets, the carpet, the spoons. The place was freezing. Why is a bathroom cold. I never knew I had a face like that. My face was bones. Cap low to the eyes. Full lips. A cut on my ear from the fight. I looked to one side directly behind me. Who was that looking at me? I saw someone looking at my eyes, my cap, the cut on my ear. Was that you looking at me just now?

While I was at the mirror I thought how I could check for my father inside me, his echo, the trace I thought of when I thought of him. Somewhere on top of my stomach. I felt under my ribs just in case, nothing, put my hands inside my skin, took out one organ at a time and lined them about the sink: liver, stomach, kidneys, heart. Nothing. Maybe the echo dodged behind my liver when I put it back, washed me inside with the soap that removed him. He must have used a disappearing soap, so much of his life he seemed a stranger to himself. And the things that disappeared? His face for instance. What hand stole it, what hand pulled that face away.

I checked the fridge for a voice and sat in the dark in case anyone was watching. I boiled water and poured a cup and held it to my lips and left it there, inside the upper lip, just where it burned, to feel the pain and wake up. The steam wet my nose and forehead. Some pain did approach, but it hung a few feet away from me, near the painting of the sea on the wall above the table.

I want to feel you inside me, come over here.

But the pain stayed where it was. It said, I'm sorry, I don't know who you are.

The steam made my eyes water, the tears thought they were from me, but when they saw the face under them as they left my eyes, they refused to fall on that face, a strange face, that is why I did not cry. My hands shook, but they shook because they belonged to someone else. I floated in one big heart that would not beat.

At midnight I opened the freezer and checked to see if the pills were saying anything. They didn't have a whole lot to say, I had consumed enough of them already. Their voices froze in their throats. If I did not visit them for a day, those throats would open again and shriek for food like little birds. I put one on my tongue to warm it up, but it slipped down my throat the first chance it got. I put the rest back in the bag and covered them with more ice to keep them fresh.

In the living room again, I switched to another news channel. A man in a navy-blue suit and a red tie was leaning across the news desk and pointing a finger at the lens with a flag watermarked on the wall behind him. The man sighed and shook his head: Terrorist sympathizers here in the US, how they're plotting against you and me. The threat from anti-American propaganda is rife, folks, rife in American retirement communities. Who are these leftists and where are they coming from. While he spoke, the top corner of the screen showed footage of jackboots stamping across a wet gray yard, and the bottom corner showed the same photograph of the old people in the home as was on the other channel. The man in the red tie continued, Foreign workers employed as janitors in our most cherished institutions, where your mothers and fathers are living out their years. You don't want to miss this. And later, the school bus situation, sexual and physical abuse of our children. No one cares. But we do. Keep watching.

I got up as an advertisement for a security firm began with a woman lying in a flimsy nightdress on her bed reading a book as a bulky burglar prowled in the dark downstairs.

* * *

When I was tired enough I went to my bedroom and sat at the window and put back on the two raincoats as well as three pairs of socks, waiting for the lights. Somehow my organs were all mixed up. The house pulled at me with a hollow sound, the rooms groped for me, told me to live in them and be happy to be alone, since that was my lot.

I said to the house, You must think you're talking to my father. My father is gone and you shouldn't be wasting time with me.

The house answered back that it knew my father was gone and it knew very well that it was talking to me. The house said it felt alone and I was the only one around.

I am on my own, the house said, though your father knew all along that you were going to be alone.

It finished by saying that I should just turn around and go back into another room and sit and wait for being alone to come and get me.

You don't know my mother then, I said.

The house had nothing to say to that.

Thoughts blended into other thoughts and slipped to one side. But sleep got delayed on the way to my body. I think it ran into a plastic bag in the freezer, the ones I had to check on after I had the conversation with the rest of the house. When I counted them before putting them back there was one pill less that when I took them out. I think because it got into my mouth. I found an old amphetamine in the seam of the large raincoat pocket and sent it in to keep the other pill company. Slow and fast, sad and happy, same things, and one after the other.

Sleep. A body drifts to find sleep. A mind floats after the body, they both part, the senses float off differently, the eyes close but the house speeds into them, the rooms switch places, my mother's bedroom is the living room, the bathroom is the kitchen, the upstairs is downstairs— and suddenly I see what has been happening: I cannot sleep, so the house sleeps instead of me, it tumbles around and tosses the rooms in its own dream and messes up the covers.

At three in the morning the pain was worse, cold blood came down the pipes in my head and sucked pain off the tops of nerves and tightened me into a bend. In the kitchen the trapped pills tried to make up for it by screaming at me to take more of them, I took the bathroom razor, smashed a fist on the razor to get the blade out of the plastic housing, there was no knife in the house, my mother sold all the knives, did she not. I got the blade and sliced the flesh of the mattress open and gouged my hands inside for any rock or crystal: one must have got away from the lot of them hiding there. I grabbed at the tissue of the fluff and the wires and found not one.

From the fridge behind me drifted the voices of the pills, the sirens in the freezer. They said that if I took more of them I wouldn't get any more headaches and I wouldn't feel bad and that I'd be free of my parents for-ever. I didn't have to feel bad, they said.

They said, Open the refrigerator door and take one of us.

I opened the fridge and carried the pills into the living room and left them on the television on top of the moving pictures. Talk all you want now. Before I said that, though, I picked another one out of the bag, put it on my tongue and felt it scuttle down. I walked the hall, whispering my mother's name.

I went to my bedroom window and leaned my face on my hands and knew I could not sleep. I was so tired that sleep itself was no longer any good. Tiredness had taken hold of me and would not be moved along or disposed of by closing my eyes, not for hours, not for days. Tiredness that was not tired.

I looked out at the salt flats, the chalk wilderness to the west, and heard the wind carry the smell across the night. Even the stars were hiding.

I lit a candle to light my face and prove to the world that I was alive tonight, and I watched the city's lights spread like a broken yellow vase up the mountainside and peter into the black. I lay my forehead on the sill, and when I woke a couple of hours later, someone had cleared the clouds away and thrown a handful of stars across the surface of the lake.

Four o'clock in the morning. I passed under the bulb in the hall and the flashing television before checking to see how the pills were doing. I had counted wrong the last time, had counted one too many. I drank it down with a cup of water and reached the front door and did not feel my hands lift the bicycle lying against the fence. I wheeled it out the gate, looked back to my bedroom window and the curtain blowing out into the sky. I saw the young boy who used to sit at the window looking for the lights, saw his young face hoping for his brother.

I had to recover those hidden gems I hid at the shore under a foot of salt. I fit the one raincoat properly now over the other, small stretched properly over the large one, and cycled to the lake shore, this time with the pair of goggles. I walked the bicycle out to the shore, then ran out onto it, threw a leg over the saddle and cycled fiercely to keep warm. There was more of the shore than I expected. The water had retreated. Or was this the right place? The place of the picnic when I was young. I was wearing the black raincoats and sunglasses and didn't have a light on the bike, drawing circles with my eyes trawling the surface. The tires rasped on the salt as I turned a circle and cycled faster, faster till my larger raincoat flapped to both sides.

As I rode along the salt I felt the moon graze my arm like a cold finger, a wet light that cooled on its way down through the atmosphere where I saw little white circles, thousands of them, scattered across the sky. I could have reached my fingers up into that pile and tasted the heavens.

Where was the place? A small bag under the salt,

where was the place? The shore kept going parallel to the road. I turned right, into the lake. The tires reached the shallow water and I rode the shallow out twenty yards. I let the bike drop and lay with one eye under the water and one eye above. I was so comfortable lying down. Water swilled in, I fastened the goggles better around my head. I needed one sense, to see for buried treasure, and after I found the bag to live simply on a small piece of earth, live like flowers stuck to the side of a hill in a breeze, a bit of clay, a bit of sun. Give me this one find. Give me back what I buried. I knelt in the water and smashed my face again into the lake with my eyes wide open and my hands gripped the goggles to keep the seal. The water trashed into currents as my arms scraped the lake bed. It must be here, this is the place the lake has covered. I felt so heavy. I spread my arms wide, my first flight, and the lake grew around me. I heard again my voice when I put the page against my mother's skin for my brother to read, what I wrote about breathing to a boy who did not breathe. To leave everything now and feel nothing, to follow my own floating, that simple. To feel nothing—not bad, not good. Nothing.

I lay again on my side, one eye above, one below. The eye above the water watched the stars flow and the eye below stayed closed and the cold ran through me, chasing the sleep out of every corner and dark place, waking me up, wake up, wake up, Sunless, and the lake pushed at me. I felt more comfortable than in all my life,

I wanted sleep and I said Thank you I am going to sleep now and I closed the eye above the water but the lake would not stop, wake, saying wake up, wake up, I'm here, wake up, I'm your mother, or it said wake up, brother, and the tea light of dawn flickered into my eye.

And I opened the eye below the water.

He was the size of a hand, the microscopic eyes, nose, mouth. He balanced himself in the currents, expert in the water, the only place he'd ever known. I wanted to touch him but froze. I looked up at a pill shimmering on the water. The cold sang through me and wrung me. I gasped and rose through the surface and broke into a rising sun.

I found the shape of the wheels and dragged the bike loose of the lake and rode my way to the shore and left towards the house. No mercy now. They had almost put me to endless sleep. At home the medicines were lined up waiting for me above the television, some coughing and clearing their voiceboxes for the wailing. They knew I could not find the fast pills, the meth. What I hid was hidden from me. They knew they would need to be louder to compete with the television, and their song was strong and tremendous. I put them back yelling and singing in the fridge, they seemed to be rocking the freezer, *Take us, take us.* They'd wreck the place. My head spun, shook, burned. I went to the bathroom, poured water into the sink and bent to wash my face.

The water dripped into a strange, so I washed that face and pulled the plug and watched it swirl away. Then I took a towel and dried the face that was mine. But it wasn't my face.

In my raincoats and boots and socks I set the alarm clock for ten o'clock and covered the window with a blanket to keep the sun out because it pressed against the glass. Then I lay on my bed. Head splitting into bones. Opened window. Stretched on my back. The cold poured in and across the floor, rose up the walls and soaked the mattress, made a blade and slid under my skin. But I should have felt colder, I wanted to feel the cold. This must be what dead is. The blood stops and settles down. The organs sit in rows, wondering what to do now, what to feel now.

I could go back. The lake might have retreated and exposed the marks in the salt where I dug the hole. I could reach in and grab the plastic.

But the pain had me now.

By the middle of the first afternoon the screaming was coming from my mouth, my organs had turned into little fists and punched each other, my blood nicked parts of them to make them jump and ran away to my brain to get away and dragged their blades along the veins on strings after them into my brain and slit trails in the tender soft parts. I pressed my finger into my head to try and prize the blades out and they only sliced in more. I held my head in my hands and screamed into the sky. It was melting away, the fast blood was melting away, a dead feeling was coming upon me, the past was coming upon me, it was coming upon me and I was all alone in this world, Brother will you help me, will you come to me.

The sun circled and went down, rose again in the window, but I did not move. I passed through the hours and did not move. My father and my mother were wiped from me. For two days a spinning head. Water on my face, a hand from which it flowed onto freezing blood an inch below the skin, this water flowed through my face and melted the blood until it shone a little up through my skin.

On the third day my head stopped spinning, but I could not find myself on that bed. The numbness was a thick blanket. My mother's voice fell down to me though it from an otherwise silent brain: We will keep you forever.

Who did she mean? I needed to find myself now. Who is the last person I remember.

Yes, that was simple. I was young, my name was James and Jimmy and then Sunless, I chose that name. It was still true.

Now I needed a voice, so I took his voice, that child who saw only what he saw, who did not see anything that was not in front of him.

But when I tried to move off the bed, the legs and arms did not obey. I sent the words to them to move, and each time those words went no farther down the legs and arms than before. I had a name and a voice, but no body. This was clear then: a child's voice does not carry far in an older body.

And it came to pass that on the day a fly entered the room without fanfare while I lay still, an ordinary housefly with a number of tiny legs hanging down and wings so fast they looked still. It tied knots in the air and made for the orange lampshade. Once there the fly dotted the bulb with a fretful shadow, punching the four walls of the room with the shadow of a large beast. And in the silent and stinking room the fly was the loudest sound. I lay as it left the bulb and looped itself many times above the bed. I followed the line of the flight and saw the letter P. The fly went behind the lampshade again and flew out and low to drone a long K above my head. I brushed it away and saw that my hand had brushed it away, that my arm had obeyed the silent words that told it to move. My arm had moved!

The fly then flew its letters to the window and settled behind the hanging curtain onto the glass, a shadow of wings on the sunny side. It bounced on the glass until I rose, because I was able to move, and walked to the window and lifted the sheet enough to see it dotting the dirt on the sill. I looked closer.

It looked up at me. I heard it sing, it was an orchestra, the way different sounds combined from its mouth or its wings, I could not locate the origin of the sound, only that the different trills and membranes worked a thousand levers to sing tiny parts into a whole melody like that. The fly looked at me with such kindness: I had never seen a fly's eyes, the huge chambers, the way the muscles twitched with feeling. But the sun was too bright and I let the sheet fall.

I walked through the house, shuffling, drinking water, stopped at my mother's room. Nothing there but a bundle on the bed, the pillow under heaped blankets. Now she was a regular at the temple, it must have been so. She would not have abandoned the house otherwise. I lit a fire and ate food that shook in my hands, but in the fridge there was silence. They had lost their voices. Or they knew that singing to me was a waste of time now. After eating I went to the mailbox.

An envelope from Pharmalak: An opening has become available, the letter said.

I called the number without delay, practiced my voice first, shaky but with few words. I need not have. What answered was a recording. I tapped in the reference number. I answered yes to the questions. The voice at the other end then gave me a place and a time. I replaced the handset and was thankful that no human had been attached to that voice.

The following day I washed and cleaned myself generally, and the day after that I left the house with the fly inside it, the fly that made me rise from the dead. I drove to the train station at the edge of the mountain range. Beyond the rising foothills lay the big cream castle where my father died for a year.

I parked the car at the station and I waited in the wind and the sun off the flat desert for the train to Park City. One car arrived and three girls jumped out with white wires coming out of their ears and waved at the car as they wandered to the platform. One looked me up and down, then they all hunched their shoulders and giggled down into cupped hands. I shifted both raincoats and placed my sunglasses higher to my forehead and faced the opposite side of the shelter. In the reflection they leaned closer to their talk:

Isn't it so great we're all at the same school—my dad can drop us off next week—I hope this trial works better than the last one—We were on sugar pills after all that trouble—My mother was furious.

The girl in the blue sweater said, I've been clinically depressed since I was twelve.

Me too, said the third who wore a leather jacket. And from her inside pocket she produced a pillbox in a thumb and finger: I'm taking these, she said.

The girl in blue read the label.

Xanax, I gave them up because of the problems with refills. I'm taking Zoloft.

I'm on Zoloft, the smallest of the three said and tapped her pink phone. The commercials on the television, I was eleven, I told my parents, That's me, depression, social anxiety, dependency.

Someone answered at the other end. She said, We're here. Yes, bye, and flipped the phone.

The leather girl moved a circle with her thumb and took one wire out of one ear. The first time I found out what I had, the doctor put me on Prozac and said I was lucky, that some people don't get diagnosed until they're twenty.

Twenty, the other two yelled.

I tried to look beyond the glass of the shelter but they wouldn't stay still and the movement attracted my eyes back to them. They must have been listening to the music as well as talking because they were that loud.

The girls and what they were saying shuffled to a bunch at the edge of the platform. Through the shelter glass I saw the train, a silent silver and glass tube, creep for us out of the city.

Don't forget, the small one said, we have a test tomorrow in English.

The train pulled up and stopped silently, a blue and white tube with large windows, one of those electric ones that used air under it.

I did not move, let them get on first.

The small one called above the music, I definitely have ADD, I may have ADHD and other developmental disorders. She twirled a blonde braid around her finger.

The leather girl said, Mine does all the learning disorders. I had a teacher in class one day, I showed him the special needs form that said I had extra time for tests, he said I didn't need extra time for reading quizzes. I called my parents.

They filed in and walked tapping to their seats in a flurry of words and wires. I went to the back of the car and looked at two heads bounce above the tops of the red seats, the small one didn't reach.

Did he get fired?

What's the test tomorrow?

Hamlet, the invisible head said. By Shakespeare.

Just Shakespeare, what's his second name?

The tall one's head was joined by her two palms in the air: They make you read stuff that has nothing to do with me.

A finger rose where the small one was sitting. To be, or not to be. That is the question. That's a quote from Hamlet.

The leather head said, To be or not, that's a question. Now one more—we need two for the test. My mother is on Citalopram, I checked the cabinet.

The hair on the blue shoulders said, Citalopram, a chemical class for depression. I thought she looked depressed when she drove us to the train.

Then the three girls spoke together, voices rising above the music that seeped out of the earphones:

I wonder what they interact with—did it say on the leaflet, you have to read those things—I went through the cabinet—the generic for Xanax is Alprazolam.

They went quiet and I heard taps as they sent messages on the phones. My head was still sore: I rubbed the back of my neck. We were going up the slope in the rails cut into a groove. I looked behind me at Salt Lake City falling into squares as we moved away, the lake extending back into the desert. I saw the angel stand on a church roof in the city and shrank in my seat. Once we cleared the slope, it was forty minutes to the Kimball Junction station at the entrance to the valley, and Park City was a quick stop after that.

The tallest head said, I think I'm bipolar with mild OCD and latent anorexia.

A hand lifted a strand of hair to a comb: Last year I thought I had borderline personality disorder.

That was last year's thing, the invisible head said. Nobody has that now.

The leather jacket moved: That play guy again, what's the quote from the play guy.

The train reached the top of the canyon and accelerated. Cars wound on the road that ran beside the track: some had ski racks on top. As the train came to the top of the foothills, the large screen flashed at the head of the car and the weatherman pointed a wand at clouds moving from the west, the first season's major storm. Just in time for the holidays, the anchor said. And now this.

The picture showed a man and woman having dinner when the woman jumped up and started screaming. A voice murmured in the background:

Are you prone to irritability or an inexplicable urge to shout at strangers or even a relative? If you experience these feelings at holidays and have no prior history of aggression, you may have a disorder known as Sudden Irritability Syndrome, or SIS. A product has been developed to alleviate the effects of this condition. Talk to your doctor about SIS.

The screen faded with a shot of the woman throwing a glass into the fireplace and gesticulating at the man trying to hold her in an understanding manner. Above me, on the ceiling, was a poster for the odd passenger who looked up while stretching or leaning back on the seat for a nap. It showed a hand reaching over scattered open books and paper marked in red ink for a phone.

Ask your doctor if Elevax is right for you.

I closed my eyes and the dark raced for me. I opened them before it got to me.

The train moved across the plateau until we reached a valley and turned into it for the last six miles to Park City. I glanced to both sides. The mountains circling the train shone white, brown, and yellow. From peak to peak the sky stretched a pale blue light like a drum. A lodge roof chimney hung its line of smoke above the trees. In the Olympic Park, people in thick red jackets twisted down the artificial ski slopes. I saw their breath mix with the sky. Cable car wires crisscrossed the free slopes, but no one was using them: not enough snow yet—so warm this late in the season. And the slope of the town came into view, houses, a main street rising to a screen of hills.

Park City, the voice in the speaker said, and the girls bunched to the door, dipping their three heads in one uneven giggle. As I waited for them to leave, I saw a dot sail into the middle of my eye and turned to see a fly wavering down the aisle, looping up and then out the door and off into the mountain air. It looked familiar. I walked to the end of the platform and stood at the start of the two hundred yards of foot-path and railings that led to the castle with its four turrets and flags tucked into the soft green rise of a slope. The place was busy—parked cars in all the rows of white squares, people walking to and fro looking at watches in the chilly breeze. I kept behind the bobbing white wires and reached the large wooden entrance door after the three of them squeezed through with one push. When I entered the lobby I saw nothing of them.

In the time since we came with my father, the place had changed, renovated to look older. Ahead of me a wide ballroom staircase wound up to the first floor. A chandelier lit the way and two stained glass windows divided the sunlight into green and bronze circles. An arrow pointed down another staircase to a darker level, the sign said Spa and Wellness Center. Along the left wall, a reception counter, people checking in, rooms available, the sign said. I went to the right, where most people seemed to drift, and passed a glass partition—a café—lines of private booths with people eating lit by a huge fireplace, and in the corners by bulbs on iron fixtures like torches set into the walls. I reached a man sitting at an organ, playing soft notes out of sheet music. Twenty steps more to another fireplace, a large grate with logs and shifting peaks of flame, set into a light green wall I saw a door, and when it opened a brief crowd and brief hands clapping in a beam of light, and it closed after the person went in. This was the only meeting I could see going on, I saw no signs for clinical trials pointing to a different room. So I opened the door and stepped inside.

Close the door, someone whispered.

A ballroom with seventy or more people and a stage up front, a man standing behind a dais and microphone, and behind him a projection of the same man, his name tag magnified: Rex. He coughed, wiped his hand with a tissue, shuffled papers. A man with a white coat and clipboard looked me up and down. I straightened the raincoats and folded my arms and leaned against the side wall.

Rex said, This morning is the final session of Pharmalak's sales representative training program. After lunch you have a break until seven this evening when, he raised a hand, we will have the keynote address by Dr. Fargoon, president of the company. After that you will be officially in the employ of Pharmalak.

In the flickering light some faces clapped and hands watched eagerly. Men in shirt sleeves, women in business suits clutching clipboards, the top parts of them only, the lower halves bathed in the dark.

Rex continued, holding a notebook aloft:

Dr. Fargoon will address our core philosophy as we move into the third decade of the century. We want to get away from this notion that you take a pill for an ailment, a sore throat, a cut, a bad heart. Medication is a companion for life, and life is indeed a very long illness. Medicine is the new food. Would you not eat food for a healthy body? Do you not want a healthy mind? Are these truths not self-evident?

In the dimness I saw people fold their arms and nod to the floor.

Rex placed the notebook on the lectern and said, As you have no doubt learned this week, Pharmalak is a unique institution, combining a private research and development corporation with modest hospital facilities for those who can afford our services, in-house luxury accommodation, a state-of-the-art wellness center, a vigorous and successful patient outreach and research program. And I can announce that we are going nationwide for phase two—

Someone clapped and another cheered, and Rex nodded and folded his arms. The room slapped waves of claps back over the applause. He waved a hand slowly—

Nationwide with phase two of what we believe is our breakthrough therapeutic drug. The magnified sweat rolled off his forehead. I saw something bob across his forehead and looked to the projector lamp.

I've forgotten the name of the product, he said, looking lost.

Elevax, someone shouted.

Rex cupped a hand to his ear and bent to the left, I can't hear you.

Elevax! rows of people shouted.

That's it, I forgot. Rex's voice rode waves of claps and cheers.

But let me tell you that soon that name will be on everyone's lips. Elevax goes on the market in six months. It will be the new Prozac. We will transform ourselves into a national institution, and beyond that to a benchmark for global wellness. When people hear *Pharmalak*, they feel better. And you are our sales team. We believe that political changes are underway, that government interference in the health industry will wane as the benefits of direct selling become evident and consumer sentiment changes. You've met the Avon Lady, you've been to the Tupperware party, now get ready for the Ritalin coffee group, the Elevax book club.

A book club, I love books, the woman to my left said, clapping at two times the speed of other claps.

Rex moved a hanky over his face. Heart disease, major depression, cancers, we leave those to the majors. What we do are the lifestyle medications. Our business model is to tweak the brand-name drugs and develop new patents. We're just the little guys here, the Wal-

Mart of the industry before it got big. Our customers—war veterans, housewives, children—they know who they are.

Rex thought a minute and scribbled on his hand. That's a good slogan, 'Our customers know who they are.'

He returned the pen to his breast pocket and pointed to something above the crowd:

Doctors are more than a signature on a prescription, they are the necessary gap between our products and our customers. Your job is to people that gap with samples. A Pharmalak sample puts the beef back in the prescription pad. It transforms the abstraction of a name into the thing itself.

Yes, someone cheered.

Rex's voice softened, Remember that no one has to feel bad anymore, that's the key phrase.

No one has to feel bad, someone said.

Rex stopped and leaned to someone at the side of the stage and nodded, wiped his forehead and held up two hands.

Now I am pleased to showcase the proposed phase two campaign leader advertisement. This 60-second slot will be shown before first-run shows in theaters.

He signaled to the back of the room.

The projector rolled and large red letters glowed starkly on the screen: THE ORIGIN OF ANXIETY. Two cave men, one small and one large, circled each other with clubs by a river. A hushed monotone over a light drumbeat as a red arrow appeared on the screen pointed at the back of their heads.

The Hypothalamus, a cluster of cells in the ancient part of the brain that creates fear, our most primitive instinct.

The arrow moved up an inch.

And the Amygdala, another ancient part of the brain. When danger presents itself, together they flash a snapshot to the conscious mind, Danger!

The small man dropped his club and ran away. The view switched to a busy city street, crowds walking a pavement in the same direction, people behind wheels in traffic jams checking watches and rubbing their foreheads. The voice said,

Such danger snapshots served us well for thousands of years, but in modern humans the Amygdala continues to flood the brain with danger warnings. The modern part of the brain doesn't know how to shut down the signal, so the primitive warning keeps flashing, watch out, watch out. Our brain is left reacting continually to what doesn't exist, a condition we call anxiety.

The screen showed a man holding his hands above his head and looking fearfully at the sky. An orchestra replaced the drumbeat. The screen changed to a cave man walking beside a man with a briefcase on the same street, both eating fast food. A more confident voice spoke as the image froze:

Elevax. You can take the man from the Stone Age, but you can't take the Stone Age from the man. Until now.

Rex appeared in the beam again, rubbing his hands. Well?

In the dark sounded one call of Yes and then lots of cheers.

We think, he raised his arms with the claps—we think we'll go with the Stone Age.

Louder claps, whistles.

Rex shouted as music started: Let's have color-coded medications based on the threat levels. We've only just begun!

A voice spoke right into my ear—Do you have a name tag?

The woman stood in front of me with a clipboard, white coat and rusty hair tied to one strand. She searched the front of my raincoats with her eyes.

What is your name, she said.

I don't have one.

If you don't have a name tag, you probably shouldn't be here.

Her hand was at my elbow. Are you in the training program, she said.

I walked to the door and she followed me. A man moved in front of the door.

I'm here for the trials, I said. The clinical trials.

Let me show you where you should be, she said, and we walked in step out the door. She pointed up the staircase. You are on the second floor, take a right down the hall, second door to the right into the reception area, and someone will help you there. Do you need someone to escort you?

I walked back to the staircase, the long and winding staircase, and reached the next floor with the man from the door after me all the way to the office. He went away after I walked to the glass window and the lady checked my name and slid me six pages to complete. I wrote my name twice on signature lines:

S-U-N-L-E-S-S.

She counted the sheets, and getting the right number she pointed to two white doors.

Go through those, she said.

I entered a room, and four people sitting in a circle looked up as the doors swung in. They weren't talking and the room was bare except for a blue carpet and a counter that ran along two sides. I didn't think they looked like doctors or nurses or anyone who worked in the building.

I took one of two empty chairs: there was nowhere else to sit. We all looked at the ground. This couldn't be the trial, but no one was going to say they'd signed up for a clinical trial for the leg syndrome or some kind of anxiety that wouldn't go away. I wasn't going to ask if I was in the right room for the experimental medicine. So we sat and wore the silence. One in the group looked agitated, a fellow to my right in his early thirties in a brown tweed jacket who kept moving on his seat. Maybe he had the restless syndrome. On my left a girl about my age read a book, I liked her perfume. The large woman opposite me had high heels on orange shoes and a wide skirt and smelled of powder. A man also very big at the waist, maybe in his fifties, sat beside her in a striped shirt, white short pants and white socks pulled from sandals to high up on his calves. He bounced lightly and tapped his hands to a tune in his head. The white doors opened and a handbag and a voice walked through:

I'm sorry I'm late.

The voice was surrounded by rouge and red hair, she wore a blanket as a triangle over her shoulders, her age was anywhere. Drawn and puffy, she sat in the last chair and dragged it a few feet out of the circle. It was a poncho draped on her, I knew the word now, and she opened the folder on her lap.

Welcome to the orientation session, she said. And welcome to Park City.

Wait, is this part of the clinical trial? the tweed man said.

Yes, she said, sifting sheets in the folder.

Isn't this supposed to be private? he said.

She shook her head and found a page she must have wanted, It's the orientation session, she said, please respect the group.

Everyone looked from her to him. Then she looked up at us. She waved her arms.

I want you to move your chairs so that there is space of one yard between each, your chairs are too close together. We need space within the space.

Everyone moved the chairs except the fellow who spoke, he stared at her, but it was the same in the end because the other chairs moved, including the folder woman's, she dragged hers too.

Very well, she said, coughed gently into her fist.

Wait, I don't understand, the man said. What has this got to do with a trial, I heard nothing about an orientation session.

I am a poet, she said. My name is Barbara Quinta. I live in the community and have published in various journals across the state. But that is not why I am here with you today. She ran a pair of glasses up her nose: I thought I'd begin with a short poem.

Christ Jesus, the tweed man whispered into his hands. Go hang yourself.

She held the page up to eye level and held her glasses with the tips of her right fingers, so that she was leaning forward with her left shoulder as if pushing through a crowd:

Nighttime in our large house, prosperous—yes—my
husband and I eating
different fruits and wine that drape the tables
and our bed, sucking—exotic—fingers searching each
other's distended
limbs. But in my hands I hold only harsh questions in
the morning:

when I should be thinking of the war against terrorism,
why instead do I drink hazelnut coffee
and stare at the squirrels?

No one said anything, they studied their shoes. A cough, a clap from the fat man. Barbara Quinta held the page at arm's length for what seemed like a long time. Maybe there was another verse.

Speaking to the page, she said, I think we should introduce ourselves. Let's take the names starting on my left.

She opened the folder and swapped the poem page for a different one, then folded her hands on her lap and glanced at the fat man who drew a breath:

I am Marlin Fenster, motivational consultant.

Next the large woman blinked twice and blushed. I'm Lehta, with an H.

Lehta looked to the man in the tweed jacket beside me. He sighed and closed his eyes: Simon.

The stares switched to me. I stared at the wall, and when no one spoke I looked left to the girl.

She cleared her throat and eased forward as she said, Jennifer.

It sounded like a question, maybe she wasn't sure what her name was. I liked her.

Barbara Quinta said Thank you and read the roster and looked up at me.

You must be Jimmy.

I stared at her. She removed her glasses and nodded, Very well. Let's begin.

The folder again, manila with lots of writing on the cover, things crossed out, sheets of paper. Out of her pocket she counted four short pencils in a fist of them.

Please take three sheets each and one pencil.

The young man said, I'm sorry, but who are you exactly? Do you work here?

My name is Barbara Quinta, and I am a poet. I am a resident of Park City. I have been hired by Pharmalak as a permanent writing specialist to conduct orientation sessions for participants in the clinical trials. I help the company make choices by encouraging people to express themselves in writing. Verbal communication is only half the story.

She said all that into the folder.

So you're not a doctor.

The clinical trial hasn't started yet, she said. That's why it's called orientation.

The silence spread across the group along with the pages and the stubby yellow pencils. Mine had a soft tip and marks on it. I scratched the tip with my nail.

What we will do, she said, is rewrite a fairy tale. I have adapted this popular exercise to suit our purposes. The twist is, how can we help our children in the war against disorders? If you wanted to help your child face a disorder, how would you rewrite a fairy tale?

Lehta said softly, Fairy tales are something a child is comfortable with.

That's exactly right, Barbara said and smiled at her and flipped through some stapled pages. Fairy tales can bridge the gap between Pharmalak and children with emotional conditions. As a jumping-off point, first let's read the original version of *Jack and the Beanstalk*:

A poor widow lived with her only son, Jack, close to a forest. She grew ill and asked Jack to sell the cow for her, but he sold the cow for beans instead of money. When she saw what he had done, she grabbed the beans and flung them into the garden. Next morning, Jack saw from his window a beanstalk growing into the sky. Even though his mother told him not to, Jack climbed the beanstalk. At the top a fairy appeared with a white wand in her hand and asked how he got there. When he told her he climbed the beanstalk, she said, Do you remember your father? Jack said that he did not. I knew your father, the fairy said, he was a good man who made friends with a Giant who came to live with him. One morning the Giant killed him and stole his goods. Pointing down a road, the fairy said, The Giant lives that way. And she disappeared. Jack followed a road to a very large house. He hid in the oven and watched the Giant hold his favorite hen and shout Lay! and the hen laid a golden egg. Jack crept from the oven and after the Giant fell asleep, he stole the hen that laid the golden egg.

Barbara Quinta closed the book and placed it in front of her: Interesting material, don't you think?

Yes, very, Lehta said.

And we have enough to form a strategy. We already have the child's attention, now, how can we direct it. Where do we take the tale? A quick analysis might be that in failing to follow his mother's instructions, Jack exhibits signs of ADHD. Or If he deliberately ignored her, he may have oppositional defiant disorder. Fine, that's fine. But how do we tell the rest of the story?

Quinta took off her glasses and leaned back in the chair, and with both arms in the air said in a loud voice:

Please write the end of the fairy tale, write what you think must happen in the real and complex lives we lead. No made-up story—the real thing.

Lehta at once scribbled furiously.

Marlin Fenster said, Do we write as a group?

No, Barbara Quinta said. Everyone composes a unique story. Pharmalak is interested in exploring endings that reflect wellness and resolution for each individual.

Fairy tales are violent, Lehta said, reading silently over her page.

Fenster was writing too now, slowly and with his tongue. He sat with his hand cupped around his pages. Simon seemed to be writing, and Jennifer too scrawled to my left. Something at last came into my head that I could take out of it and write down, and I joined the company of moving pencils across pages.

After a while I glanced at Simon leaning into his folded arms, eyes closed. Jennifer wrote for a while and then went back to reading her book. Marlin and Lehta were still writing when Barbara Quinta pointed to her watch.

Everyone, that's twenty minutes.

I held my pencil in my palm and folded what I wrote.

Who would like to be first, Barbara Quinta said.

Lehta's hand went up between *to* and *be*.

Thank you, Lehta. Please read your writing to the group.

We sat while Lehta breathed heavily a few times and patted her chest. She read:

Jack and the Giant meet on the ground and acknowledge their differences. The Giant voluntarily climbs back up the beanstalk, and for his part Jack agrees to climb up every week with some of the golden eggs. They agree to respect each other's boundaries.

Everyone waited for the next bit, but that was all she wrote. Marlin Fenster nodded and said he liked it, went to clap and stopped, rubbed his hands instead.

Barbara Quinta nodded. Discussion of the piece? Reaction, comments anyone? After a minute or so she said, What specific suggestions might you make to Lehta about her piece, what one thing could she do to improve it? When no one responded, she said, And please remember that we are critiquing the writing, not Lehta herself.

Jennifer examined her hands, the outside of them, where I smelled the perfume most, very subtle, a ghost perfume. Maybe it was the shampoo in her hair. She was attractive and I could not say why, nothing to point to and say, This.

Simon stared at the far wall above his folded arms, his legs stretched in front of him.

Barbara Quinta twirled her glasses as she spoke: Lehta spent twenty minutes composing the piece and she did offer to be the first to share, so I'm really hoping she won't be left in a state of unresponsiveness.

Simon said, It didn't sound like a fairy tale to me.

Marlin Fenster looked surprised and raised a finger. I don't agree, he said. I loved the way she developed what happened emotionally at the end, the boundaries thing, that really got to me.

Thank you, Lehta said, and kept her face turned away from Simon.

And Jack gave the Giant something at the end, Jennifer said.

Barbara Quinta replaced her glasses. Very interesting. Now Simon, could we hear what you wrote.

Simon held his page high in the air at the ends of his thumb and index finger. It had only one line on it. I couldn't read it, too far away.

Jennifer's eyes were sharper: He says he doesn't like children, she said.

Another silence. Lehta said that wasn't a fairy tale. Simon did not take his eyes off the wall.

Any other comments on Simon's piece?

Jennifer hunched her shoulders and lifted a hand. I'd like to read mine now. Just so you know, everyone, this is really about me and what has happened to me personally.

Marlin Fenster leaned his chin into his hands.

And this is a poem, Jennifer said, so you have to imagine it's a story:

> You are not my daddy, I hate you daddy. You drove
> me like a new car,
> I told you things, you used them against me on
> hot nights,
> you taught me to make secrets, necklaces
> out of secrets. The hotel you live in or the battered
> car you live in
> in what state you live in will never be free
> of my hate.

Just so everyone knows right now, Marlin Fenster said, that is so important what Jennifer just did, she took something that's far away and she brought it to where she is at this particular juncture in her life.

I agree, Lehta said.

Jennifer turned to me, Can you show us what you wrote.

I passed a page to her, which she read at once: Jack scrambles down the beanstalk with the hen and the Giant follows him and Jack chops at the tree with the ax and the Giant falls head-first to the ground and is killed stone dead, no commas.

But that's the original ending, Lehta said.

Barbara nodded and looked unhappy. That's not an improvement at all, she said.

That's pretty depressing, Marlin Fenster said.

If it even happened, Jennifer said. But I don't believe it did anyway.

Letha shook her head, But where's the positive reinforcement, what kind of message are we sending to our children?

Barbara Quinta checked her watch. We need to move along, we have only so much time this morning.

Marlin Fenster rattled his pages: My turn then, I guess. Now what I have here, I need to explain this first.

He put the pages on the floor and sat up and shifted to the edge of the chair, I'm launching this new program in the fall, it's based on some things that this tale reminded me of. Now, if we look here. He circled both hands to his abdomen above the hips and to the side. The liver, I think the liver contains a lot of unresolved issues. In my program we focus on the liver, get the liver up and running with nutrition and meditation, and then move on to the next organ. I call it Trans-Organizational Therapy. The therapy focuses on organizing your life and getting that moving as a whole.

I love it, Lehta said.

My slogan is: Put the organ back in organization. Anyway, in my piece I saw that the Giant may have had some liver issues, but I couldn't quite get it down in time, so I decided to explain it instead.

You've admitted you've got nothing to read, Simon said.

Well, Simon, I think I just did read something.

I understood what he was doing, Letha said.

Barbara Quinta said, I want to thank the group for participating. We have one more task. Fairy tales are copyright-free, and everyone trusts a fairy tale. Pharmalak will issue a special edition of *Jack and the Beanstalk* next year as part of its plan to reach out to the younger population. I am the editor. We want to insert writing exercises in the back of the book. If what the child writes suggest medical help is needed, a parent can contact Pharmalak using the contact information provided. So what do you feel are the relevant themes in the tale? Let's get this done in ten minutes, I know you want to move on.

The war against terror, Lehta said. We must protect our children.

Quinta said, I see. So perhaps a question, such as 'What is threatening our country?'

Yes, but more specifically, Marlin Fenster said, 'What is threatening *me*.' Remember, it's the perspective of the child we're concerned with here.

'What is threatening me in my life,' Lehta said. That would be a very good question.

Barbara Quinta wrote briefly in her notebook. Very good. Another question?

Lehta spoke again: 'Do I have disorders that I would like someone to take away?'

I saw her in my eyebrows looking around for support. Nobody made eye contact. She continued, And why must we call them fairy tales when they are about murder and child abuse. We must ensure stories in our libraries show how everyone is unique and everyone is equal.

Simon closed his eyes, I don't understand how everyone can be unique and also equal.

That's right, Lehta said. And why did you close your eyes when I was talking.

I can't close my ears.

Lehta said, I knew it—she gave a little bounce and turned on her seat—I took it as a disrespectful mannerism while I was talking about my life and my feelings. You have disrespected me.

Marlin Fenster rose to his full weight on the sandals and the socks followed, pulling up tight along his legs like cones. He sat down again. I'm hearing just a little, he straightened his index finger and made the bottom of a triangle out of his thumbs, dysfunction. Pressing both palms down as if hoisting himself, he said, Why don't we get with the program here, people? He shifted on the seat, hunched his shoulders and looked around the group. Are we okay on that? We need to focus here and not sweat the small stuff, work together. He drew a large circle in the air with his hands. Not lose the big picture.

So we disinfect the fairy tales, Simon said. Go to the library and rip those offensive words right out of the pages.

Lehta said, Especially when children are going to be exposed to them, children you don't like, so what do you care? In the meantime it would be better if we could discuss with the child the disorders as they happen in the tale. Those are the questions that need to be in the back of that new book, she said.

Simon looked at his watch, leaned back and sighed.

Barbara Quinta nodded.

So, Lehta, what is a disorder, Marlin said. In terms of your experience, I mean. He shaped his hands around the question.

She said, Disorders are when a person experiences a thing that they have not caused that makes them function wrong and stops them from being the person they can be.

Marlin Fenster turned to the group. We need to get that in writing. Did we get that?

What's this? Hey what's this? Jennifer turned over the page I gave her. She must have seen the other writing I did on the flip side.

Look at this. She grabbed for the other pages on my lap. Let me see the rest.

Simon said, What?

Jennifer said, I want to read this.

Barbara Quinta looked at her watch. I'm afraid we don't have time.

Simon said, You said ten minutes three minutes ago. That leaves seven minutes.

Jennifer read the pages:

A story about a new ending. A mother and a father went to a hospital one day, and the mother gave birth to a boy. The boy was born seventy-six years old and was brought to intensive care, because being old he had problems with his swollen heart and kidneys, his knees and his ankles. A lot of babies did not last the first year for that reason. But this one did. They called him Andy. They took him home and took good care of him. A nurse lived in the house for the first six months. After two years he was able to walk on his own, his back had straightened a little, less of a hump, and his heart improved enough that he didn't take so many tablets. The kidneys worked so much better that the transplant could be cancelled. After five years Andy was walking briskly and was off the heart medications. When he was born he mumbled things that made no sense at all, but after six years Andy took in his surroundings without effort and commented on issues with clarity and precision. He remembered more than he forgot. Ten years into life, Andy was sixty-six and play-ing tennis in the courts downtown hitting as many balls as he missed. He found himself occasionally looking at women in the other courts, and often he had a drink with someone who caught his eye. His skin grew softer and tighter and his back kept straightening, almost no curve. His parents were happy that Andy had made it this far, but soon they took him aside and told him that he had to plan for the coming years, nothing urgent, but could he give them an idea what he wanted to do. He said that he did not know. At fifty-five he had gained a lot of muscle and his head was covered with more black hair. He drove around town in a red car he bought with his first year's savings from his new job, because he still lived with his parents and he was able to save. Andy found himself stopping to talk to women more than before, they excused themselves a lot and said they had to be somewhere else. That went on until he was fifty-four, when one woman seemed to bump into him wherever he went. He found his own apartment, they began seeing each other, and at fifty-one, Andy got married. All was well for another ten years, but as he was turning thirty-nine, Andy felt something. He was running every day, had never been stronger, his waist was thin and his eyes were clear. But something was wrong. Without telling his wife anything he took long walks on the shore and wondered was this all there was—a leaner and healthier body, a clear memory, living with a lovely woman—was that going to be it for the rest of his days? The years brought more worry without a name that, when he was twenty, turned to dread. His many friends never spoke of it, but he sensed that they shared the same thoughts. He drank in bars and found himself asleep at the wheel, waking up at dawn in the driveway of his house. His marriage ended. By the time he was fifteen, Andy was inconsolable and did not know what to do with all the energy he had. Ten more years passed, and he had never felt so alone, so cut off, so misunderstood. He was smaller too, and less able to lift things. At five he went to bed and stayed there most of the day watching a television he barely managed to prop on the dresser. No one helped him. At two he tottered out onto the street and started on the road to his parents' house. His father was dead, his mother was not. He spent the last year and a half of his life there. In the final months, Andy was not able to talk and cried for milk, that was all he did. In the last day of his life, Andy found himself lying near his mother. Two hands lifted him inside, and he could not breathe, the suction was stunning, it pressed all the memories out of him, the life he had just led, and he found himself in water, his eyes closed, his tiny heart beating. And nine months later, Andy disappeared.

Simon looked at Jennifer. That was written on the sheets?

She waved them. Yes, he wrote that.

Barbara Quinta looked pale through the rouge. I don't see a connection to the fairy tale exercise.

Simon laughed. Of course you don't.

Well if you're so smart, Lehta said, you tell us what the connection is.

I'm happy to, he said. They're both about wanting a better life, and they both never happened.

Barbara Quinta pointed to her watch, Forty-five minutes is up, she said. Thank you all very much. She took her folder and wafted out the door.

The receptionist behind the glass came in: Take an hour for lunch. Here are your lunch vouchers.

While we examined the green vouchers, through the walls of next door we heard the murmur of a familiar voice: I'm sorry I'm late. My name is Barbara Quinta.

In our room, everyone stood to go. Marlin Fenster and Lehta said they would have lunch together. Simon slapped me on the back as we walked past.

Well that nightmare is over. Are you having lunch?

I was hungry, so I said yes and rose to go with him.

Jennifer pulled at my coat sleeve. Can you wait?

Simon shrugged and said he would meet me in front of the building. He had to have a smoke, he said.

She leaned her perfume close and whispered though we were alone in the room: I'm an alcoholic, my father abused me as a child. Do you live around here?

I glanced to my side and behind, did not see anyone else Jennifer could be talking to.

I do not, I said.

She stared at me and dragged her chair closer, her eyes thawed into drops. Her lips quivered. Were you abused too, she said softly. You can tell me everything, anything.

I said, Nothing happened to me.

I'm in recovery, she said, making a question of the last word.

The legs of my chair had wrapped themselves around my ankles. She was so pretty.

Do you write like that all the time, she said.

I can't write, I said. All I did was say it in my head first, then I wrote down what I said. That was me speaking, not writing.

She said, So you wrote it because I was here. Something you wanted to tell me. You must have a secret.

She leaned close, her lips brushed my ear, her golden perfume was in my eyes. Tell me something.

The chair would not let me go. I had to say something, so I took what had been in my head when I wrote the new ending.

I said, My brother was not born, he lived backwards and his birth was the end. We lived separately for some reason. I never saw him before he went back to being born.

That's so sad, she said and met my eyes.

She held the pages and pressed them to her face, reading them through her skin. I saw her closed eyes fasten tears to the edges. I saw the touch of sparkle in her hair, I saw the brush of the comb across her forehead, I saw the curl that would never stay in place because it was grown too strong one way, I saw the way her lips could not close and be relaxed, I saw her shoes pointed straight forward when she sat, I saw that she was kinder than she wanted to be.

I told her I had to go and walked along the corridor and down the staircase. I hoped my mother was in the house again. She was with the temple people or she went to Chicago to visit friends. Perhaps she really did want to go live there again.

Outside, Simon lit up. I needed a cigarette after the fairies upstairs, he said. He dragged the smoke into his mouth, blew it out again, swept it away with his hand, bowed down before me and said, Thank you.

For what?

I was all alone in there until you showed up. I saw you in the raincoats and felt better.

What's wrong with you, I said.

I don't have the money for the drugs, but I do have the restless leg problem. I kick the sheets to pieces every night, it's like a dance hall down there. I saw the ad for the trial and drove here from Missoula. How about you?

I don't have the money for drugs either. I wanted to build up a supply.

Fair enough.

Around us the walkway was busy with coming and going. Another train pulled in with a bigger crowd, families, business people, people holding skis. The mountains had enough white but at the top, someone could ski along the peaks but not down the slopes, the snow didn't reach, not the year before either, someone said. The clouds were catching on the peaks like thread pulled loose.

My bet is for rain, Simon said. Too mild. He shuffled the pack at me. I'm going to have another one.

I'll see you in the café, I said.

He pointed over my head, I'll be right along.

Through the big wooden doors I went and past the staircase and along the right hall and into the café I went. I called the house from the lobby. The phone rang in the kitchen, it rang in the kitchen, up and down the hall, the rooms. I waited for my mother's hand to lift it and for her voice to reach me along the invisible wire between there and here. The line went dead.

Behind the serving counter in the café, I saw a tiny poster between the beverages menu and the bread oven.

I read what was on it as the man poured my coffees:

> Constantly forgetful? Can't remember where you left the keys? You may be suffering from Accelerated Memory Deficiency, or AMD. A new product may delay the onset of AMD. Mention Elevax when you talk to your doctor.

With the two coffees I sat in a booth near the back in the unlit part, the shadows jumping in front of the fireplace on the floor. This was the intended atmosphere then of this part of the café, to eat in peace. The crowds sat in the other three quarters. Two women stood in the center and looked about them with trays, one looked at the booth next to mine in a line of empty booths in the darker part. They sat down and I felt the seat bend behind me. A voice punched words:

So then I thought it might be some kind of CGAD.

What was that?

CGAD, Chronic Generalized Anxiety Disorder.

Really. Why?

I avoid social situations, I can't relax when my son's friends visit, I hate waiting rooms.

If those are the symptoms, then I have CGAD too.

I want to treat this disorder. I want to try this new thing, you know how you wish you could fit in more. I don't like missing out on my son's life.

You could have ASD: Aggravated Sensitivity Disorder. It could be that. What if it is and you get treated for CGAD instead?

The punching voice said, Listen, will you, I don't have ASD. I have GSAD. Anyway, the medication for both of them is the same, so it wouldn't matter if I was given the wrong diagnosis. It would be the right cure. That's the miracle of modern science—you can be wrong and you can be right at the same time.

Her friend said, Just in case it's neither condition, Give your son some space, you can't run everything. The disease might be a variation of SIS, or a combination of CGAD and ASD, I don't know one from the other.

That's just the thing. I've been keeping up. So I know. It has nothing to do with how I treat my son. What has that got to do with anything? I am nervous for my own reasons.

All this talk made me anxious, the last traces of the crystals in me, not screaming since I got on the train, but whispering, still whispers and sometimes stabs. I fished in my pocket and found nothing, groped then in the pockets of the larger coat underneath and found a group. I placed a Double X in my mouth before it could shout, and half-a-one followed it. I was cutting back. I was cutting back. The women next door talked until the talking floated off into the center of the café, the talking put the trays on the tray counter, and when their voices were completely gone I saw the café swim in the general silence after them.

A shadow arrived. Simon slid in.

I came straight to the dark part, he said in the flicker of the distant flames. And here you are.

Simon looked about the café. Yes, I can see there are a few of them here.

He pointed, He's one, she's one. They always come alone.

Who comes alone? I said.

He leaned across: Mormons. They all come alone. They lead the perfect life, he said, quoting his fingers around the last two words. And it never is. That's why a lot of them end up here. Suicide, divorce, anti-depressants. Utah leads the country. You live a lie, it comes out somehow. They had me for six years: I got out. They tried to get me back for about a year, calling to say hello, why don't you come visit us, no pressure of course. But if you go soft, they move in the artillery: eternal hell. You have a devil inside you, an evil spirit, you betrayed their friendship, come back and we'll just talk.

He sat back again. Thirty-five miles away and they feel close.

I said, They came to visit my mother.

Tell me she's not one of them, Simon said.

I don't know. She might be in Chicago. Tell me the story, I said.

What story, Simon said. I don't have any story.

You know, the one in that book. They gave her the book. I think she still has it. She hid it.

You mean *The Book of Mormon*? Ask your mother, Simon said.

Why not you? I said.

He was quiet. Maybe the story was still inside him,

telling him itself over and over, for so long that he could not go anywhere where the story was not. I wanted him to explain to me how a story would not stop talking inside you. Then I would know what my mother was feeling.

I said, One day when she was gone from the house I found the book under the bed and read it.

So why, he said, glancing around, are you asking me to tell you what's in that book then? His voice fell all the way through the sentence until it was a whisper.

I said, It was a story of how a man and his family sailed the ocean to America. Everyone is always discovering America, so it made perfect sense. America has been discovered by lots of different people. I think soon we'll find out it was never discovered first by anyone.

Simon nodded as the pain in my head sharpened. I did not have a lot of money. I needed something for the pain, the scratching in my brain.

I said, What I read was this: A man called Lehi was living near Jerusalem and it was six hundred years before the birth of Christ, but he did not know that. An angel with wings appeared and told him that the city was about to be attacked. He told Lehi and his family to go away, he would tell him where to go soon. Lehi and his family and possessions traveled across North Africa until he came to a big sea. There the angel whispered to him and he built a boat. Lehi and his family sailed the sea, carrying what he owned and brass plates carved with Egyptian writing—the history of the Jews.

After a long time sailing west he landed on a coast. They all built houses and had children. Lehi had two sons, Nephi and Laman. Nephi was good, Laman was bad. Laman took off and set up on his own. Nephi stayed with his father. Both groups got bigger and they started to run out of room. The Nephites and the Lamanites started to fight each other because there wasn't enough space. The angel turned the Laman skin a shade of black to separate them from the good part of the family. That way the two would not mix by accident. The American Indians and the Aztecs and the Incas were Lamanites—they were Jews—but their skin was stained red because they fought with the good part of the family. It was red or black skin, a shady skin. Even that did not stop the fighting, and it might have made it worse. The two groups fought all the way up this strange land where there was no history and they ended up in a place where New York was going to be a long time later. But they did not know that. More fighting for a long time. The bad people wiped out the good people. An angel told the last leader of the Nephites, his name was Mormon, to carve the whole story on gold plates and bury them in a hill in New York. He did. Soon he was killed.

And that's the story. I sipped the coffee and sat back.

That's more or less right, Simon said. What did you think when you read it?

A lot of detail, I said.

He said, But did you believe it?

That's a good question, I said. But I don't think I understand you.

He said, Did you believe it? That it happened?

I liked it. I wanted it to be more like *Jack and the Beanstalk* so I could believe it. I liked the horses and the carts and the farming and the fighting though. With those details, it had to be true. Why all the details if it wasn't true?

So you didn't mind horses being in ancient America, he said.

Simon hadn't touched his coffee and he didn't touch it now.

Finish the story you began, he said.

I said, My mother told me the rest one day when my father was at work:

In 1820 a man called Joseph Smith had a vision. An angel appeared to him in New York and told him that there were gold plates hidden with a history on them. He had to wait for a few years, and then the angel appeared in another vision and pointed to the hill where the plates were buried.

He dug up the plates and put special seeing stones like hens' eggs into his top hat and sat behind a curtain and translated the Egyptian on the gold plates into English. The Book of Mormon. That's how we know all this happened. Mr. Smith told the story to settlers from Europe who were living in New York. They followed him to Missouri because the gold plates said that the Garden of Eden was there. The plates also said that

Christ came to New York, appeared near their houses, and that they could be gods of their own planets in the next life.

Simon sat forward, That's correct, all of it. But what's not in the book, he said, is that Joseph Smith brought those people from New York to Missouri and they set up a community that only traded with themselves. When the locals drove them out, they moved to Illinois. When Smith's wife caught him with another woman, he revealed to the senior members that God told him they should have many wives. A fourteen-year old girl married him at some point. The people in Illinois weren't going for that, so he ended up in a jail cell in Carthage. A local crowd freed him and his brother and dragged them out into the street and killed them both.

Do you believe those stories, I said.

Simon shook his head, Rumor is the perfect weapon. You speak a few lies and watch them fly along people's mouths until they're true. It must be true if so many people say it. And why couldn't Jesus appear in America if he could rise from being a dead man? As for the lost civilizations of early America, archeologists dig stuff up all the time. Maybe a civilization is all waiting under the ground, the lost civilization of early America, everything they were waiting for discovery under the ground.

I thought about millions of people under the ground waiting for discovery.

I said, Joseph Smith translated the story into English from behind a curtain. It must have been a magic curtain.

Simon said, Nothing is magic in this world.

I said, What other explanation is there? The story must be true. My father brought me into a church in Chicago when I was young. You go into a box divided by a wall with a window in it covered by a curtain, and you sit down on a bench. The curtain slides back and you tell a man you never met before, who is on the other side of that curtain, certain things you did or thought. He listens and nods. At the end, he asks you if that is everything, if you told him everything. You say it is. He then tells you that to get the stain off your soul, you have to repeat certain groups of words a number of times. If you do, what you did will disappear from inside you. The bigger the stain, the more often you have to repeat the words to get rid of it.

Simon nodded, Now I feel better.

A man with sunglasses sidled over to us from the next booth.

I was listening, he said, because this is the quiet part of the café and my consultation was over early. I had time before the train. I have something to add to that story.

Simon said, It isn't a story.

I believe you, the man with the sunglasses said. It fits in perfectly with what I've been saying for years, what I told my doctor today, and he says there might be something to it, but that I should take the medication anyway until we find out one way or the other.

They had me for twenty years. I got out, spent three years in therapy. I'm negative and I live near here.

Negative, I said, moving the cup, the trace of a question in the word.

Negative like the old cameras. I live in the negative imagery. I don't like discussing it. My life has changed. For instance, Australia doesn't exist. That's the negative image of Australia. Get it?

I looked at the table.

He said, I'll make it simpler. The future doesn't exist, the future is a continuation of the past. How to be sure you never get anything. Put it in the future where it's safe and it will never happen: Tomorrow I will be happy. I will be happy next year. I hate my life. I don't even like myself. But one day things will be different. Get it?

The man adjusted his sunglasses: There is no future, only the present continued.

I said, What about Australia?

The man with the sunglasses said, That's historical. You have to go back to disprove Australia. Remember the sailing ships? The 1700s, all those adventurous people creating problems. The government suddenly says it has discovered this big place far away, lost of sunshine and open spaces, and of course all the adventurous types want to go. The government says, Of course you can go! And those people sail off and are never heard from again. People get letters saying how lovely it is, and more strong people want to go. The government says, Sure, you can go! But no one ever comes back. They were really sail-

ing to an island off Scotland probably where they disappeared. End of strong people, government gets to rule,
no opposition. Australia is a myth.

Simon said, But the satellite photographs of Australia
we saw in school.

The sunglasses turned to him and the mouth smiled:
Who owns the satellites? Come on, you've got to be
smarter than that. How come Australia is so like England?
How come they play rugby so well? Those are English
rugby players playing in a studio in London, and the
whole thing is bounced off a satellite.

Simon stared at the sunglasses as the man continued—

Even true things are rearranged. Just one example:
JFK's assassination. JFK planned the shooting, he wanted to take a bullet in the shoulder to get the sympathy
vote in the elections. But Oswald slipped and blew the
president's head off.

I did not ask who JFK was.

The man said, Fine, I wanted you to know. Don't
blame me when you disappear.

After he left, Simon sighed and spoke into his hands:
I studied economics in Edinburgh, and in London I studied economics—the science of human behavior. It didn't
get me far, did it, but I do know that man is wrong. A
government doesn't control citizens: citizens do it all by
themselves.

Simon pointed to the far end of the café. See that
man talking to his child, Do you want this, let's do this,
let's play this? He isn't talking to her, he's talking to

everyone else. He's saying, 'Look at me, I am a good father.' People create communities that don't really exist. They want to control each other's lives so much that they end up controlling their own and have to take medication. I wouldn't be here except for my restless leg and because I have no money.

My coffee was cold and I was out of money. It was time to go.

Simon seemed to sense my thought. I'm only visiting the area, he said.

I said, In that case, I live right outside Salt Lake City, a few miles along the road. You can come stay with my mother and me.

Thanks, he said, but I'm staying in Salt Lake City. I'm visiting my friends. I attend the services in the temple and so on, but as an outsider. I've told them not to expect anything more.

He pushed the coffee away. He had not taken any of it.

I watched him and knew the book was doing its work in his blood even when it was closed and not being read. Some books you don't have to open. They read themselves to you even in your sleep. They fill your senses with words. The book had brought him back to it in his sleep, back for more words.

He said, There's something temporary about America. It's like you're always visiting.

I had no idea what he was talking about. I had never visited America because I never left it.

Shortly we went upstairs. Outside the blue room, the

receptionist in the glass told Simon to go into the room with the others.

She said to me, pointing to the ceiling: The fifth floor, take the stairs to the elevator. You will be seen by a specialist.

I went back to the ballroom staircase and took it to the next level and saw three dark green elevators in a row with leafy designs of 1, 2, and 3 carved in gold above each. I went to the first and pressed the button, the only button. A woman in white shoes glided with a tray down the carpeted hall. The elevator door slid open and I stepped inside and pressed the number 5, the only button. As the elevator moved, the noise slowly increased behind me: on the rear wall of the elevator the screen showed the RX-24 Health Channel icon in the bottom right corner. A man with a furrowed brow sat beside a window beyond which children played on a swing.

Intolerant of children, noise, social situations? Often wish you could be alone? You may be suffering from Aggravated Sensitivity Disorder, or ASD. Talk to your doctor.

I turned right out the elevator and walked along a burgundy rug to a waiting room, long white couches and long paintings.

Is that Jimmy? Someone called from above.

I followed the sound up a short narrow winding stair

to the fifth floor and an open door. I knocked and walked in, the tidy woman who met me raised her hand out to where I should go, it was larger hand than it should have been. I walked a green carpet to the strange and purple door, such a famous doctor that he didn't have *Doctor* before his name on the door, just *Mister Fargoon*.

Come, the voice within said.

I stepped inside. His office didn't look like a doctor's office: the light was low and soft, bookcases lined the walls to a window with the mountains in it, the train station five stories below, the houses dotting the lower hillsides, the gray clouds hesitating on the peaks, bending the sunshine. I was in the turret, this was the single window under the flag. A mild green plant reached to the light from a polished oak desk. Mr. Fargoon wore a white linen suit and a blue tie and did not look as I walked to the armchair in front of the desk and saw the drawing of a fish on the wall behind him. No sea, no angler, no sky, just the fish, and not what type.

Fargoon opened his folder. Please sit.

On the mountain slope a copse of trees lay about five hundred yards away, and above it two hikers wound their way up a mountain trail to the summit. A stain landed on the window, a watery-white stain, and I saw that the sky had less blue now than cloud. One passed across the sun and the desk lamp shone brighter, it became the sun of the office.

What big eyes Fargoon had, or big glasses I mean, wheels of glass with two spokes curled around his ears. He looked a bit like a fly. If I threw some crumbs on the table, would he feed. His eyes were pins inside the lens, as if he didn't look at things but stuck looks into them and stared at the looks as they wriggled.

You're the last man, he said.

I said I was happy about that.

No, I mean you're my last man.

I said by way of saying something, Will you be going straight home after me then?

I can't, I'm giving a speech to the sales reps at seven. But you are my last patient.

I felt the first fringes of annoyance at this repetition. I longed for more of what was in my pocket.

I said, Am I supposed to say something about being the last one?

Fargoon stood and smiled broadly under the glasses till his thin lips stretched into split red hairs under his nose. Then the thin lips trembled:

You are my last patient ever. After you, I am no longer a practicing psychiatrist. The technicians will conduct the rest of the final trial, a wrap-up really, for six weeks. I usually interview one participant on the orientation day, and I chose you, my young friend. And that means you will get the first sample.

He sat and pulled the top off a fountain pen and dangled the nib above his first question.

He said, Are your parents alive?

Not my father.

What did he die of? What disease?

Lack of health insurance. That was the name of his disease.

Fargoon's fountain pen moved across the page, much longer than my simple answer, and I thought about the strange man earlier in the day who pronounced that there was no future, only the eternal present. My father, even when he was alive, hoped for a future where he could be healed, a future that would wait until I caught up with it. Then my answer was wrong. Hope was his disease.

Fargoon finished writing. Now, what are your symptoms?

As he waited for an answer I cast my thoughts across the symptoms a man might have with these conditions and herded those thoughts into a sentence:

I kick the sheets to pieces. It's like a dance hall down there.

Does it wake you, he said.

I don't sleep.

Would you describe it as uncontrollable leg movement for more than five minutes at a time for more than three times a week for more than three weeks?

Yes.

Does it increase anxiety?

I said, I want to fall asleep and cannot.

He said, But does it increase anxiety?

I nodded and ached with the lie of the movement.

He said, Restless Leg Syndrome. That wasn't too bad, was it? Have you always been thin?

I can't eat properly when I can't sleep.

The scratch of Fargoon's pen curled the ink into letters. And then the scratch stopped: he was staring at me.

Because you look pale and tired.

The fountain pen lay on the desk sideways and he leaned back. I needed to change the subject, those eye pins were sticking into my thoughts and might burst one. He might see the desert, the meth lab, the sediment of the meth in the bed of my shallow thoughts, the battery man buried in Wendover, and the good Doctor Mister Fargoon might lift the phone and ask for the police, say that he had some information. Another Xanax is what I wanted, never mind the name I made up, I wanted it by any name. One more makes it two and a half for the day—or else find the half and make it an even two. No more after that.

Then I fingered the half, the rough edges were unmistakable. I slipped it out and coughed it into my mouth, my hand there for politeness.

Bless you, he said.

I am being followed by a fly, I said, after I swallowed. It was not entirely true, that statement. I didn't know what the fly had been up to for a couple of days.

The pins in the glasses did not move, his body swaying lightly in the reclining chair.

A December fly, I said.

Fargoon allowed himself to lean forward.

And what did this fly reveal? he said.

That it is not a fly.

What does this possible fly look like?

It looks like a fly, a household fly, nothing fancy. Legs and wings.

Why is it following you? Fargoon said.

It is more like a thing traveling with me. I was lying in bed sick and it flew into the bedroom. It wrote letters in the air, but I missed some. I could not read the script.

The fly seemed to interest the famous psychiatrist, a flicker moved his face. His pen moved in small circles, not flowing from left to right.

That's an astonishing story. You clearly do have restless something, a restless head perhaps, he smiled up at me. But it may as well be your leg.

My leg is not my head, I said.

Fargoon shook his head. The answer is Elevax. It doesn't matter how the particular symptoms of anxiety express themselves, it's all anxiety. Anxiety can mask its ways among us. We could be here forever. The answer is the same.

I'll try it then.

He smiled. I will prescribe you the first Elevax. I will give you a sample and a prescription for a further two months from our pharmacy, and a technician will follow your progress. Congratulations, Jimmy. This one had your name on it all along.

Out of the drawer he took a white container with *Elevax* written in slanted green and placed it carefully on the desk between us and sighed.

Elevax is a wonder drug, he said. Before this, finding out what was wrong with a person was like swinging a hammer in the dark. Sometimes you hit first time, one prescription. Or it could take a few months, a few years. He rested his chin on his hand. Even a lifetime. Would you have been ready for that?

I said, Ready for a lifetime?

To identify your disease. He smiled, What a difficult question for any of us to answer, I'm sure. Well, no need to have to answer that now. You are looking at the answer.

His fingers touching the container, both palms upward.

I stared at the Elevax. Even if I wanted to say something, what was the point. Another voice bleating out his insides. So I went straight to the point.

What's it made of? I said.

What? he said.

The Elevax.

I held it and looked around the box for the writing: What are the ingredients? Does it take long to make?

Fargoon said, I don't understand.

So he was going to keep it to himself.

Rain spelled sunken words across the glass, words I could not read, the letters sliding into one another. Outside, the pitch-black mountain under a big cloud moved by wind across the valley. A flake hit the window and turned to water. I decided to ask in different words.

I held out to him the pages from the Elevax box. Can you read to me the story of the tablet?

The story? You mean the information leaflet?

I said, Where you find out what happens after you take it.

Fargoon sighed. He unwrapped the book and opened it into a map across his two arms. He tipped his chair back and spoke to me through the creased fan of the page:

Elevax is used to treat anxiety. This medication is thought to work by increasing the activity of the chemical serotonin in the brain. Anti-anxiety agent. Anti-depressant. Anti-obsessive agent. Anti-panic agent. Post-traumatic stress disorder agent. Social anxiety disorder agent. Side Effects: Drowsiness; trouble with thinking; problems with movement; fast or irregular heartbeat; fast talking or excited feelings or actions that are out of control; fever; inability to sit still; low blood sodium causing confusion, convulsions, dryness of mouth; lack of energy; serotonin syndrome (diarrhea, fever, increased sweating, mood or behavior changes, overactive reflexes, racing heartbeat, restlessness, shivering or shaking); unusual or sudden body or facial movements or postures. Other side effects that may occur usually do not require medical attention: Decreased appetite or weight loss; headache; nausea; stomach cramps; tiredness or weakness; trembling or shaking; trouble sleeping; agitation; anxiety; blurred vision; constipation; increased appetite; vomiting. Other side effects not listed may occur in some patients.

Fargoon reached for a tissue and wiped his hand. That's it, that's the story. That is the disclosure.

I said, Isn't it strange that anxiety is a side effect of medication for anxiety?

Not really, he said.

And why are they called side effects and not effects. Are they off to the side?

Fargoon stood and walked to the window. You are the last patient. This is a rather special day for me. May I be candid with you now?

He turned to me. I hope I can say that I was once candid with a patient. May I?

Yes.

He placed a fingertip on the glass and leaned into it. I'm afraid it's all chemicals to me. An emaciated woman looks in the mirror and sees only fat, she doesn't see the bones sticking into her hips or her elbows, so she starves herself on that day too.

He tapped his knuckles word for word on the desk and spoke as if though the window glass to the mountains outside.

Reason means nothing. You have to change the way people feel, and that, my young friend, is what chemistry does so very well. Talking about wounds opens wounds. We are nothing but accidents: I will name a few now— depression, sadness, regret—these are emotional chemistries, and by our chemistries we shall fix them.

Neither of us said anything for a long second. Fargoon coughed as he arranged the fountain pen to write.

It's interesting, he said.

What?

For a fellow who doesn't talk much, you have me doing it. But this is a rather special day for me.

He pressed a button: Bring me in some coffee, Mabel.

Another flake came to rest on the window, but this one stayed. I looked again. Then in the window, the fly appeared. He met my gaze unflinchingly. The kindness was gone, or the light had changed and made it seem that way.

I wonder, Fargoon angled back in the armchair again, I wonder how much of it is fear. What do you think?

Fear? I said.

Fear of what can happen. Of what may have happened already.

Those pins in the glasses were fixed on me.

I said, I don't understand fear.

His voice drifted, his glance drifted to the window.

I think it was one of the ancients who said that fear cancels out every other emotion. Every other emotion disappears when fear is present.

I am not afraid, I said.

Then where is your mother? I thought I heard him say.

He seemed lost in the window and muttered something.

I said, What did you say? She is with the temple people or she is in Chicago.

He sat straight again and said, I'm sorry, I remembered something just now. He rubbed his hands: Very well. A mix of lithium and anti-convulsants. The essential properties of Elevax. You asked for the ingredients. Now you have them.

He looked about the office. Do you know that I haven't had coffee today at all? My wife keeps telling me to give it up.

Will you give it up?

I tell her I will, but not when I feel a speech coming on. He tapped his watch. I have a speech at seven this evening.

He stood and asked me to stand with him.

Your group rejoins at four. I want to show you the phase three posters. We have them from the printer. I've hung them already, we'll use them later in the campaign. He raised a hand: Come, let me show you out.

We left the office and walked toward the thin stairs, along the ice-green walls did we walk, and on our left we passed three posters. One showed a young girl standing under a cloud with a caption underneath: *Feeling depressed?* A few steps farther, the same girl stood under bright sunshine, and under that one was written: *Feeling high?* The final poster showed her split into shadow and light, the left part of her mouth down, the right part up.

Fargoon said, That's our phase three marketing campaign. We don't mention the name of the product and there's no slogan in the third poster. It's a different strategy.

The receptionist drifted toward us along the ice-green paint of the walls and handed Fargoon his drink.

He said, I came up with Elevax myself. I analyzed names going back thirty years. *Zo* sounds like so, *loft* is part of lofty, a subliminal so high. *Pax* is Latin for peace, and *il* sounds like ful, which leaves you peaceful. For my part, I combined *elevate* and *relax* and made out of them *Elevax*.

Fargoon stood back and admired the posters. I thought there didn't need to be a name for any drug. Call it by the disease itself. Sadness, Anxiety, Anger, Panic Attack, Rage. If someone suffers from rage, call the drug Rage, and for later versions put a number after it, like Rage-4. If you annoy people for no good reason, talk to your doctor about Obsessive-3.

Fargoon tapped the third poster with an approving finger.

Elevax, he said. Keep your eye on that one. As we discover more lifestyle diseases, we'll adapt the drug. I'm certain we'll be seeing ten spin-offs. Our vision—he said.

Vision? I said.

A drug for every mood.

The narrow green hall crowded in on me. Fargoon drank from his cup.

I said, I have a slogan for the mixed-up girl poster.

Fargoon straightened his blue tie with his free hand under the poster of the split girl.

What is your slogan? he said.

'Paranoid Schizophrenia is when you make two of yourself in case they get one of you. Talk to your doctor.'

He laughed. You're an odd fellow, Jimmy, but I'm quite sure that's the attraction in you. But that's both a rare and an old disorder and not the focus of the campaign. Did you remember to bring the Elevax with you?

I heard the new voice from inside my pocket say that it was indeed there: a different accent, more mature than the squealing Xanax. I was glad to hear it.

Yes, I said.

We passed the national flag that stood at the top of the fat staircase. He stood under it at the top of the steps and turned to me.

As my last patient, let me give you some advice from the lips of the ancients. Fear is the greatest poison, certainty is the greatest pain. He settled his big glasses: a flag is a cloth version of a drug—play some music and hoist it, and if taken with a gentle breeze, people will feel the surge of chemistry fuel their beating hearts. Quite simply, they feel better. The anthems of the world are medicine, and we have replicated them. These are new truths. Nationalism and religion are nothing but reactions to a threat. That's why you always find them in the same sentences spoken by the same people. If they only understood biology.

You must read a lot of the philosophers, I said.

Why that's generous of you. He fingered his huge

glasses, Yes, I do read the ancients, Lucretius, Cicero, the letters of Seneca. When I can. In any case, I am liberated today, no longer the reluctant psychiatrist. I am a free senator in the Forum. He waved a hand, So what did you think of the phase three posters?

I like that they don't say anything, just the pictures. But I have a question, I said.

What is your question?

Could you get restless leg syndrome if you wanted to travel but can't do it because your wife is sick?

As if I said nothing at all, he leaned close and whispered closer, You're not one of them. I can tell these things. You see, when we decide to be honest, we can be honest.

He turned and joined his hands:

You are not one of the temple people. They sell control of the afterlife. I sell control of the present life. The same rules apply. It is fitting that you, the last man, are the first.

He rested his hands on the balcony and arched over it and looked down at the people milling about in the lobby. He spoke, a strangely shrill voice from the railings:

Some people will believe anything. I'm talking about what you take for what you want to become. The magic wand is chemistry, my friend.

And looking down at the crowd, he said, I think you will feel better after today.

I didn't see how they could have heard him. He

shook my hand and we parted. He went back to his office. I went down the steps.

At four o'clock I went to the white doors and opened them an inch into the small room with the blue carpet and saw Jennifer, Marlin, and Lehta at a table. Simon must have left. On the table were a bowl of snacks and plastic cups.

Happy Christmas everyone, Marlin Fenster said, lifting a plastic cup.

Happy Holidays, Lehta said, raising her soda. I think we should toast the troops.

She had gone from *I* to *we* in one sentence. I envied her that.

Yes, Marlin Fenster nodded, his arm around her. Happy holidays and let's support the troops.

Downstairs again, I took the walkway to the train station. It was time to go. I had my drug for thirty days, and after thirty days I would not need my drug. I was sure about this.

Down the ballroom stairs I went, the long and winding stairs, through the lobby with all those people filing left and right, checking into accommodation for the Friday night or going straight to the restaurant, shaking hands and mentioning the warm weather. I checked my pocket, the big raincoat pocket, the right one inside the small raincoat, the few I had brought with me milling around in that pocket, one of them had run onto the inside lens of the goggles, which I also brought with me, and I trapped that one with a fingertip but let it go. I mixed with some people walking into the restaurant and sat with a boiled herbal tea in the booth. At that point the previously trapped pill found my fingertip again, ran into it.

I brought the chosen one up and then it floated for a second or two on the brief lake on my tongue before it joined a river down my throat.

The man with the sunglasses appeared, he talked about the moon until he ran out of moon to talk about while I watched from my booth the sky through the slit of window above the serving counter, and soon he watched too, silently, four eyes in total fixed on that turbulent sky.

Night was mixing with day. I could not delay long. I could not let night fall and be on this mountain. I ran along the walkway to the train station and ran my eyes up and down the timetable. The next one left at four-fifty, thirty minutes to wait. I glanced about me in the glass-walled shelter. The old town of Park City at the end of the platform to the right. The main street ran long with houses, restaurants, a cinema, a bookstore, surrounded on three sides by smaller hills with houses. West lay open ground, the condos in horseshoes, one behind the other, rows and rows of bungalows with orange roofs and lawns cut to a tight green. The high glint of the last sun brought me back to the castle, it sparked one window, the turret window where I saw a tiny Fargoon looking at the sky. Something tiny flew about his head, I saw it despite the fraction of space it occupied in the office. He looked to it lovingly.

Too many rays of sunshine came out of one large low cloud, rays like spokes. There, that cloud, that cloud moving toward me, the wheels roiling vapors. What trawled the sky and the mountainside with its eye: *We see you, Sunless*. And the wheels spun the rays of light through the cloud as it came to the center of the valley. I blended myself with stillness under the frames of shelter. The cloud reached the station. I should have read books more and been ready for this. But all that fell from the sky at me was bits of the sun, bits of the last day covering the world and covering me. I saw the left side of the sky, still fine and sunny, the right now dark and almost night, the cloud was drawing a curtain across the valley from side one to the other, night pulled by a chariot and that angel with the sword that had followed me all the way from the temple by the lake.

Park City yellowed with the Christmas lights on Main Street, they would spread under the night a false day between days. On the opposite side of the street the orange light of a bookstore slanted over a woman in a chair onto the pavement, a bird flew over the roof, two birds. Someone crossed the window with shopping bags. I thought of living in a world lit only by the moon and the stars.

The wet snow had stopped, but now there was a coating on the ground that the wind couldn't blow off. I looked fearfully at the sky, the wide and open sky. The chariot moved slowly overhead, plowing the cloud as it passed with a shrill and grinding noise. Then I saw the wires, a cable car hoisting itself up along them to the mountain with people inside, that was the chariot.

Fifteen minutes for the train.

The Christmas tree at one end of the street glowed yellows and reds, the passing glow of shuttle buses. In the streets, people clapped their hands together and smiled. One or two pointed up. The snow fell: brief, large flakes, as the mountain and Park City turned white. Little orange streaks in the sky flashed through pieces of ash. The castle with the flags grew bigger, sun streaks flitted in and out of deep mist. Was this strange sky, that orange glow out to the west, was it also down the mountain above Salt Lake City, was that city on fire, the Last Days, had the angels poured the bowls of plague. If so it was too late for me, only the bad remained, the good people had all disappeared. They had fallen up and were gone.

Five minutes until the train.

I imagined Fargoon again looking out of his lonely room, imagined him running down to me outside and taking me from the train and upstairs to talk to me about his sadness. Then he walks me out of the office and down the small stairs to the railings by the ballroom stairs, turns to me and spreads his arms out wide, and I see the people downstairs mill around his body, the fireplace, the old furniture covering a new building. Fargoon says, I built this castle on the American dream, says it with the broadest smile covering everything inside him.

The man at my side asked me was I going to Salt Lake City, did I live there. I nodded. He said he had some things to show me, that he had a special message for me, he had a briefcase, but I turned away from him, took my father's goggles out of my pocket, and put them around my head for seeing stones to read the prescription for the pharmacy in the castle: *Elevax 10 mg*.

The train slid under the glass, and on the train I walked right and sat in the corner of the last row. The dark was trolled across the valley and the lights in the window rows of the castle were all that remained of the shape. The train rolled out of the station and in a second the castle was gone. I closed my eyes for another second and the dim light of the turret window gleamed under my skin, under the eyelids, and I saw the beating wings, four feet long, filling that high window, and I heard Fargoon with his wings spread out trill beautifully all the orchestral parts of a song divided on his tongue, issuing timbers across the delicate membranes of his sipping tongue, his trembling lips and the casket violin of the torso shaking the trembling vines of his song into the sky and lacing cracks across it, and the cracks grew to fissures, and the heavens broke through and dots flew down, they spread wings and I saw more pour through the cracks, fighting their way down, cries of anguish, stabbed flies, victorious flies magnifying south to the ground and spilling upward frantic before they hit. And I saw another mighty cloud come down from heaven, pierced on the right and on the left side with silver wings. And under the cloud I saw legs glow as if on fire, and then the wings fluttered and the cloud parted, and I saw a rainbow in the shifting vapors. I saw that its head was a mighty circling eye flashing in the sun. And then two legs pierced the cloud, and two more, until the cloud disappeared and a winged creature hovered. It held a little scroll in one of its legs. I approached and pulled the scroll from the pincers at the feet: *Thou shalt have no strange flies before me.*

I woke from a sleep, a minute or an hour of delicious sleep, an orange cold and juicy inside my head. Soon the train reached the end of the mountain range and the yellow blanket of Salt Lake City appeared below me rolled across the temple, the town square, the houses along the foothills, the wide straight streets that turned into one road that ran west. The moon rose above Antelope Island and the white salt desert I could not see.

My face leaned on the window by the seat as the train rode slowly down the canyon. I felt the cold glass. They had worn off, the crystals were wearing out of me completely, only the slow pills now, a dreamy mind. The whistle blew and I stepped out, the man with the briefcase too.

Excuse me, he said.

I said it was all right. But he meant something else.

He opened his briefcase and held some pamphlets and a book. I recognized the book.

He came closer, May I share a spiritual message with you.

What, I said. Are you a Mormon?

No, I am a Church of Latter Day Saints member, LDS member for short.

LSD. That's a drug, I said.

I was looking for one car in the rows of parking, and from the platform they looked the same.

No, LDS, you heard the wrong order.

I said, Is that the community of Joseph Smith, the vision of the angel, the gold plates, the special seeing stones to make the translation?

He paused with the book in his hand. Yes, and this explains how to live a happy life on this earth and to pre-pare for a happy life to come. We share a very simple message to begin with, a beautifully elegant message.

He was pleasant and had the feel of many years of patient learning about him. I had nothing against him, but I had nothing to say to him and no room to hear anything, at least not now, not when my car was nowhere to be found and I was getting cold. So I repeat-ed to this man what the sunglasses man said to me in the restaurant the second time he appeared. I remembered the words exactly, though I had paid them no particular attention at the time.

I said, The moon landings never happened. We really went to Mars. The moon was interference. That film of the first step onto the moon in 1969 is fake, it took them twenty takes in the studio because the actor in the space suit kept falling off the ladder. One small step, but twenty before he got his line right, and even then he got it wrong. You see where I'm going with this?

Since the sunglasses man had said all that in one breath, I copied his manner of saying it. The man placed the book and the pamphlets back into the briefcase and shut it. Meanwhile I finished the rest of the story: So the government has the entire world glued to television sets while it places a communications center on Mars.

The briefcase man shook his head. With respect, I don't think that's possible given the technology of the time.

I could not find my car. I would have to walk into the lot and along each row to find it. I turned to him as we approached the station gate and told him what the sunglasses man might have said,

But the gold plates and the seeing stones and the red Jews and Jesus appearing in America, those took some technology, and I believed you.

The man tried to walk faster and said, I have to go now. I really don't have time. Some other time.

I kept up with him because I did not want to delay him.

I said, Angels are flies.

At the gate out of the station the man turned—Look,

I don't want to talk to you. This is not a good time. I'm very busy.

I found the car after walking past it twice. I drove silently through the streets of the silent city and reached the road to my mother and father's house by the waters of the shallow lake. I thought of Fargoon alone in his office after the speech and writing at his desk with pills falling out of his pockets, streaming out his nose and mouth, the porridge that would not stop streaming out of the pot, the same story my mother read to me once out of a book with pictures in it when I was still in the crib. I wanted to stay with the thought of my mother reading to me in that crib. I remembered briefly and clearly the smell of her skin even when I closed my eyes and I heard only her words to me in the dark. But slowly Fargoon mixed into the story and the porridge pills swam across his desk instead, piled to the edge and spilled off and clouded the floor and inched up the sides of the walls, they spilled into the corridor and down the thin stairs, filled up the large staircase below it, filled up the venue halls, the waiting rooms, sprayed out the large wooden door of the castle and flowed thickly in sludge down the street, covering Park City, the trees, the slopes. And then came the first news reports of rising yellow pills up the mountainside until a lid snapped shut, and all the pills were resting for the day. On the television the pills recited the news, they handed over to more pills that talked about the news, and the first pills said, Thank you for the news, and now this important message.

The swish of the road under the tires, drops of rain on the windshield, the wipers lazy on the glass. It was raining in Salt Lake City in December. I wasn't feeling that well at all.

Ahead in the house, the pills in the refrigerator summoned a tiny sequel, just one, they were out of breath or sleeping. They said people just can't do that, stop after months of taking them, that people can't do that, it was dangerous. They somehow knew what was in my mind. They said it was dangerous again.

Too late for that, I said. You can't fool me.

I parked the car at the house and walked to the door. My shoes clung to the sound of the water all the way to the key and the opening door and the dark hall. In my mother's room I saw the same arrangement as before: no mother.

I splashed water on my face and left the house and walked over to Mr. Swan and knocked on his door. Mr. Swan, on his own for the seven years since Mrs. Swan died. On his own like me.

A minute or two later it opened. When his watery eyes saw me, he leaned heavier on his cane and pulled the hem of his sweater down as if preparing for something against which he had no defense.

Mr. Swan, I said. Can I come in for a minute.

He looked down as if trying to answer a very complicated question and walked ahead of me, switched the cane to his left hand and kept to the right wall of the hall. Someone had come and filled the room with green plants and a single white table where another plant draped shoots. A new television with a chain on it sparkled in the corner. But the room was cold for someone his age. He sat carefully, eyes fixed on me.

He said, I'm surprised to see you.

I said, I was hoping you might have seen my mother in the last couple of days.

He tried to talk so hard his cheeks wobbled and some spit splintered his lower lip.

I saw her.

What was she doing when you saw her? I said. I had a few hours to go before the pills wore off in me. All there was after that: Elevax. I was frightened even before I could feel the fear.

He looked at his feet.

Would you like to come over to the house and watch television? I said. I have a fire burning.

Swan looked from me to his television and to the floor. Okay, he said. Can you wait?

I helped him to his bedroom, a bare place with a bed and a table, two shoes at the bedside. I gave him his coat out of the closet and put it on him because he could not lift it across his shoulders. We took the cookies and the tea he liked. The walk took five minutes with rests to let his breathing catch up with his steps.

Inside my parents' house, I sat him down by the fire

where my father used to sit and watch another television. I saw Swan try not to look.

I stole this television from you, Mr. Swan.

I know, he said. It has a channel, this television, that the new one doesn't have. I like to watch this channel. He shook a hanky out of his pocket and dabbed his lip.

What channel is it? I said.

The one with the documentaries, the history.

I clicked through the channels for him until I reached it. He immediately said, That one.

I gave him the remote. He held it like an old friend.

How are you holding up? he said.

I thought for a second: I'm better. I'm back to what I was.

Well that's good, he said.

In the kitchen I made him the tea. As for songs in the fridge, nothing. All I heard were the guns coming from the living room, and when I walked in I saw the explosions light up Swan's face.

My mother, Mr. Swan.

He paused and said, I saw her a few times after you left.

After I was gone? Was she looking for me?

In a way, he said. She came over here the day after you left. She said she knew you'd come back, she was sure of it. She brought a cake and some wine with her, and we lit a candle on the cake, it was her birthday, and then she showed me pictures of you and your father when you were young. She was lively, the way she used to be before, you know.

I nodded.

He said, I brought out my 1940s records and she danced with me in that red dress she wore, with a ribbon in her hair. Of course I could hardly move, look at me, I was standing with the cane, so she danced my part for me too. We talked until well after midnight, and I fell asleep. When I woke in the early hours she was on the couch, curled up. It took me ten minutes, but I brought my coat, what I'm wearing, and put it across her. In the morning she made me breakfast.

Go on, I said.

Swan nodded. She was so happy. It was three days in a row she spent here. I don't think she went back to her house except to check if you'd returned.

I said, What did you do the second day.

After breakfast she showed me all the same pictures again, what you were doing, how you did at school, the notebook you kept and what you showed her in it when you were young, the pictures you drew, the Blue Jay. She liked what you wrote about the Blue Jay. When evening came she grew quieter. You know she never took that dress off, and some kind of perfume, it was quite lovely. The second night she slept on the couch again, this time with a blanket, and she sang me to sleep with songs.

And the third day?

Swan coughed. She left in the afternoon, she was worried, I could tell. I thought it was because of you. She either stayed with me because she was happy and wanted to be with someone, or she wasn't happy and wanted to be with someone. It can be hard to tell the difference.

He placed his eyes on his slippers and then on me: You know?

On the couch I stretched my legs out like Simon did and folded my arms. The fire was pleasant. It would be nice when my mother got back. We could do this, sit by the fire and watch the television, not this set, but maybe Swan would give me the cheaper one he had now for his own one. I could pay him once I got a job. And Swan could sit with us. I regretted never asking him over: two houses, lonely people everywhere.

Swan fell asleep and I watched the Normandy landings, soldiers floating to the ground in parachutes, tanks bursting through hedgerows. Ninety days to break out of the beach and move inland. He woke up in a documentary on the Battle of Midway, planes rising off the decks, the carriers had to turn against the wind so they could get the lift under the wings. Smudges of smoke dotted the sea.

That's a good one, Swan said. That one is very good.

He lifted the remote and the volume went up. I've seen this one maybe fifty times, he said.

I said, Why do you watch those films?

Swan did not speak, and I did not repeat the question. I was following the rest of the story when he did say something:

I'll be ninety-five next year if I make it. On the afternoon of June 20, 1944, I was twenty. It was after

Midway, the one we're watching, he pointed to the television. It was the Battle of the Philippine Sea.

You were in that battle?

I'm the last one, he said. They're all gone. All the men who flew in the night to find the carriers. I'm the last. I wasn't the best pilot at all, better fellows didn't make it back. They were fine boys, they were great boys.

What happened, I said.

Swan took the tea and placed his heavy eyes on me, as if they needed to rest somewhere, there was so much tiredness in them, especially if he was to talk as well.

I get the order mixed up, he said. I once knew the order. I forget the details a lot.

He spoke slower, measuring not the words but each syllable, as if he was spooning each syllable into a glass:

I flew a Hellcat, mostly a fighter but with room for bombs. We were ordered to fly late in the afternoon, our boys had spotted the Japanese fleet, right at the edge of our flying range, but this was the chance to get them. We wasted no time. The ships were like sticks under the cockpit, they had officers then who watched the sticks sail down from way up and steered in time to avoid them. But I put a thousand-pound bomb right through the deck of a carrier, down through two floors into a hanger and I saw the planes dance on the deck, that's the sign. We turned away, no real formations, just getting back any way we could. I saw a Zero pilot dive into the sea for a torpedo that was heading for their flagship, he flew straight into the water in front of the silver tube, it blew his plane and him to bits, but we sank it anyway.

I turned for home and hoped for the best. On the return journey I was flying into the wind, a gallon of fuel every forty seconds. I brought her a little low to the water to get that extra lift just above the waves. In the second year of the war they said you'd have the radios filled with guys yelling out instructions and pilots yelling back what they were doing, but by 1944 it was mostly silence, a few commands, a quick response. So the mostly silent radio wasn't much company. It was a fine evening, out in the Pacific. You see the earth, you see the curve. You're flying a tube with wings shot through and bits coming off around you, oil leaking. Those two wings are all that's between you and drowning, and if you make it back, in all that endless water, there's this little heaving splinter you have to land that plane on. Then it got dark. Landing a plane on a carrier is bad enough in the daylight with the heavy roll and pitch, twenty feet difference in a few seconds up or down. You sort of crash the plane onto the deck and hope one of the arresting wires catches the hook.

But the night was down and I was on a very big ocean. I was watching the fuel gauge like it was my blood. All I had was an engine and the sound of my thoughts, what I would do if I made it to the carrier, where I would live after the war, I went through the places, the towns, what kind of house, the girl I would most like to marry if she'd have me, the kind of job a man like me could get. An hour later I start hearing voices, the voices of my friends in other planes strung out god knows where in the sky saying calmly that they were going in, they were out of gasoline, not shouting or yelling, a few words and the radio goes silent, then a minute later another few words from another voice in the night. I sat there and listened for the engine to start spluttering, imagining the boys going down, seeing them in the cockpits, skimming the waves then nosing into one wave and tumbling into bits at a hundred miles an hour in the black water, the cockpit gets jammed, a man is hammering at it from the inside and the water reaches his head and the plane tilts a few feet under the water. It had happened before: standing on the deck I'd watched a man drown in an airplane.

I'd about given up when the lights came on. They lit the horizon. The carrier had lit its landing lights. I was two miles away. All the searchlights lit the sky like all the houses we grew up in where switching on the porch lights and guiding us home from where we'd gotten lost. It meant they could get a torpedo if a submarine was anywhere near, but those lights came on for us, for me. I put the plane onto the deck and the wire caught the hook and the plane jerked and stopped, I felt myself and knew I was alive. I could breathe and it meant I was breathing. We lost a lot of men that night, they were never found. They went into the sea and disappeared.

With Swan I couldn't tell, I thought I saw him cry, but there was so much wet on his face all the time.

They're all dead, he said.

He looked to the picture on the wall, except that it was the wrong house and there was none on the wall he was watching, but with Swan he could have seen it anyway. I remembered it in his living room, an aircraft carrier, a photograph.

The Enterprise, he said. I think of her every day. About thirty years ago they started dying, the ones who lived to an age where a man falls ill anyway. One by one they went, and when I could I went to the funerals. I can't go anymore, and there's none to go to.

I said, Tell me about them, your friends on that ship, who were they.

Swan's eyes filled. I can't, he said. My story is out of time.

He tapped his chest. He spoke with more long pauses:

My mind forgets the order of things, the faces get mixed up with voices. I don't want to lose what I knew then. Life was never the same for me afterwards. I came home after the fight was done and I thought I could do anything. I could be whatever in life I wanted to be. We fought them with our hands and teeth island by island half way across the planet and we won. I came home, I swapped one set of clothes for another, I got ready for the rest of my life, what I promised myself in that cockpit if I ever made it back to the ship. I married and found a job. Susan was a lovely woman, but the days went by and the months went by, and I settled in. Somehow I lost the feeling, I got defeated in so many insignificant ways. A dollar short, always a heating bill behind. Small things, money for clothes, money short through the fifties and sixties, even in the good times. Maybe it was in me all the time. Maybe a soldier fills a purpose, but it's not enough to fill a life. Some mornings I could smell the defeat on the way to work, why was I doing this, why have I not won those dreams yet. My cockpit dreams got replaced by other people's dreams, my wife's, my daughter's, college, finding money for this and that. I don't doubt that they earned them more than me, but I wish I could have those days back, he said. I was so afraid of dying—and so afraid I would never live like that again.

He held his shaking thumb and finger to a pincer: and I never did. I was this close to death, and I never felt so alive, so fast, so clean and strong. He clenched a shaking fist stained with purple blotches, sharp knuckles holding up the tent of his skin. Now I've lived long enough to be the same distance from dying. This time I don't mind.

I could not think of anything to say, so I said nothing.

Swan fell asleep and I didn't know it for a minute, he didn't move either way. The man said more than he should have. I got my mother's blanket and put it over his shoulders.

When I woke it was late, ten-fifty by the wall clock. Swan was looking at me in the same position he'd slept in.

Mr. Swan, I said.

I'm fine, he smiled. I know you're tired, but I have to tell you this about your mother.

I know, I said, she's most likely with those people downtown. Or she's in Chicago. She'll be back.

Swan's eyes changed, though again nothing in him moved.

But you must know, he said quietly.

Know what, I said.

He said, She went into the house. I saw no lights. When she did not come to visit the next day, I dressed myself and made the journey to her. I knocked on the door, I thought I heard her calling, but the door was locked. That night I called the police.

He pointed behind me out to the black lake. She was out there, lying face down in the water. She must have fallen asleep in the water. It was cold and quiet that night. She must have gone out for a swim to wake up, and she somehow fell asleep.

Swan's eyes briefly met mine.

Where is she? I said.

She has a place in the cemetery. That's where she is.

I could see he wanted to touch my arm, the distance of the few feet to me was something to be planned and mapped, every step and rest, he could not simply walk. So he said across the space to me instead:

He said, I took care of the expenses, all that. I had the money in the closet, I knew you were off somewhere and that you knew, of course, what had happened, but I didn't think you'd be back. The police will want to talk to you, give you the report.

The floor disappeared under me and I fell. My stomach and my kidneys and my heart floated down with me, there was no skin wrapping them, and I fell under my heart and my stomach in that black space with no wind or air, nothing I could breathe. I fell far under them, and saw the other parts of my body not falling as fast and knew that what I could not feel remained above me with them. Swan moved on my left side as I passed him and I stood in the kitchen and felt nothing there too. I felt nothing because I was not in the kitchen, I was falling in this new place that looked like the old one, but the old one was gone, and the new place was the shadow of the house my mother and father and I lived in. It could not be the same living room. Swan shrank until he was a dot. I took a pill from the raincoats, it knew I would be back. It said it was about time.

I lay on the kitchen floor for a while. I tried to remember what I saw when I came back from the desert. How did I not see that she was gone when I came back? But I did see that she was gone. What more could I have read into that? I was not myself. And that blinking light on the answering machine. I remembered seeing that. What message waited in there for me?

The message might be from the police. Not sad news of an accidental drowning where no foul play was suspected. No: the message from the police was to ask me to keep an eye on my elderly neighbor who kept calling them because he could not find where he left things. He could not find his cookies, he could not find his slippers or even his television. Now could not find the woman who lived next door.

He remembered one thing he did find, *The Enterprise* when the captain ordered the ship's lights switched on. After that he kept losing things. The world filled with things he could not find. And the true ending of the tale came to me, what I could not write for Barbara Quinta before: Swan had escaped the bad Giant and made it down the beanstalk. He landed on the ground and ran home with what he brought back with him to set up a new life. But his mother did not recognize him anymore. He tried to tell her he was still the same boy. I don't know who you are, she said. And his friends, they said the same. He tried to explain that up in the sky was so different that he could never explain what he experienced there, what he saw, what he felt, the colors, the speed of everything. Nothing he said helped. He did not belong on the ground and he could not go back up the beanstalk. And so for the rest of his life, Jack lived a little bit up in the sky. The price of winning was losing what he had before. Swan and the Beanstalk.

From out of the letter slot in the front door, a thousand miles away, I was sure it was from there, I heard the rustle of the night talking. These words I could swear I heard: Your mother is waiting for you. She is lying under a tree that in winter is as white as china, that in summer moves under singing birds. She has never known rest like this.

I walked down the hallway, past the living room and out the door. I walked in a circle about the house, round it twice, three times. From inside the window I saw Swan's head flash in the television as he watched the war. I left him to his joy, even if he was waiting for me to return.

I went right on the road toward the yellow lights of the city.

The rain stopped, the wind swept the stars about the night in brushfuls, they appeared here and there in patches of clear between clouds. At about quarter of a mile I turned and looked back at my parents' house. The living room window was out of sight. I thought of Swan and his head watching the television, I would watch television with him tonight, I promised to sit with him. Upstairs I could see the window with the face that looked out so many nights to the lake, wondering where all the people he lost had gone. Sunless, a name as good as any for what any name does. One name could do for just about anything. My name is Sunless. I have a brother I do not know. He never had a future. It never came for him.

I knew where my father was. But I had never gone to see him after the burial. The fear had chased away every other wish and kept me to itself. I did not visit him.

I shivered, it was cold, and a thought slipped into place, for a second, though it fell out again and leaked into others. Was that a thought, something on its own. Running from the headache, I raced myself down the highway, spread my raincoat and tried to fly.

Fly, Sunless, race yourself and make it there while you can still move, make it there before the sun comes up.

I fingered the prams in my pocket.

I stayed to the side of the road, out of the spray of passing cars. The city was ahead of me those few miles, I walked to the lights and left the dark desert behind me, I walked between rain showers falling hard and brief, I walked without the notebook.

I wrote four simple words in my head as I walked: What is a father?

His name was Paul. I could draw a picture of him. The eyes, the jaw, the neck, the mouth and nose, the ears and hair, the forehead, the shoulder, the lines and the eyebrows, I could fill those things in. But what then? There had to be something under the picture, some words to describe what I drew: a father is a voice, I heard it before I saw—a father is a hand, it held mine when the world could not stand straight. And when I was older, his voice bridged the longest distance with a word. What I knew about him. How he dressed, where he worked, his name, the words his father tended to use more than others, the ways he was kind and happy and angry and fed up and how sometimes he was none of those things. If I wanted to bring people, show them who he was, how to do it? Here's my father now. There's his smile, his walk, there's his sense of humor, those are his disappointments, this is what he worked at, over here is his memory of his own parents, what he thought about me. All of him is here. He used to be there, he used to be in the house with me, but that was then. Because one day I woke to a silent voice. The voice was not mine, so I went through the house to find it, I'm fairly sure I did. I searched one room at a time, the places I heard it talk before. I heard the missing voice from an armchair, from under a lamp, I heard the missing voice from in front of a silent movie. The missing voice was coming from all sides.

My father will turn up one afternoon and tell me that he had in fact died but that it was all a mistake. Or he won't. There's no other possibility. He and I sit and talk for a while in the kitchen or at the edge of my bed, and he tells me what he felt and saw in all that darkness, but first he wants to know if he can live with us again. We talk about it for a while. He says that being dead has changed him, not because he has changed, but because it changed us, and he is different to us now. I say that we can all be different too, all change together.

I was a mile down the road and walking faster. I think I was outpacing the pill, the Xanax could not take hold, could not dream me, I was fastened to the ground in the wind and the bursts of rain and cracked another on the goggles and let it rest under the tongue, where it moved away.

I tried to think of him as a photograph, the image a person is in the mind. What could I remember of my father without a picture to remind me. After he died, he burned away in my mind like a page when a match is struck and held flaming to it. The brown rust advanced across the white page, and bit by bit, his body collapsed. The hands went, because they were at the edge of the page. The top of his head, scarred down to the forehead, then his face, all scorched. I knew for a moment how most living people go invisible: they drive to work, return home, watch the television, go to bed, and every day there is less of who they are. More is burned away.

If I could not say what my father was, I should at least say what he could have been, what we might have been, in time. My father lived an unobserved life. He missed Chicago because he had more to do there, and my mother missed what he missed, that was the way her love was made, it was made for him, she was a swan and there could be only one other for her. But she would not leave this place. It was my brother who kept her here. After she went to bed, my father stayed up late. He lived in a dream, so no one really saw him when he undressed for bed, listened to the radio, read a book, dressed for the day, went for a walk. No one saw him watch television, light a fire, fall asleep in the armchair. I did not see him, he was at the edge of sight where I placed him every day. No one saw him lose his friends to bad stomachs and bad hearts. No one saw his friends grow thinner and fewer than his fingers, like Swan's friends. No one saw him rush to the phone when it rang at 3 a.m. to hear a voice, turning on the television to hear a voice. If he could have lived a few years more I could have stopped being a son and he being a father. My father and I could have been brothers.

The walk lasted two hours. The mild weather was driving the showers from the west in front of a shoving wind. There was rain and then there was no rain, and again and again.

The graveyard gate was closed and padlocked, it glistened in the drops. How can a graveyard be closed? What are they not doing in a graveyard that they do when they are open. I jumped the wall. Across and down, the aisles and lines of stone, large and small, drifting in and out of the quarter moon when it stuck out through a cloud. The lawns sloped down from the higher foothills, and standing there I saw the gleam of the lake beyond the still and quiet city, the stone blocks that contained the living.

The two pills were talking inside me now, the flow was better, the world sank a little.

Since I never knew my own father, since I did not even know what he was, I wondered how I could find him now. I go to the gravediggers and say that I am looking for the grave of a man I never knew. The one in the red cap pulls the cigarette out of his mouth and shakes his head.

I know nothing of a man of that kind buried here. But we can check the registry if you like, at the office. He points up the hill to the small brick building with a chimney and smoke coming out of it.

I say, I'll look for a while first.

Wait, he says. When did this man die? Was it this month?

Over a year ago.

He nods and puts the cigarette back in his mouth and the shovel in his hands.

But there were no gravediggers, no minders of the cemetery. I strolled the avenues of names, even checked the new plots and saw the crosses and monuments cover the rolling field in all directions, spreading to the skyline, bunching up against the city in the distance, with all those people lying under my feet, the paper of grass. I had a moment to think how so many people could be dead in one place. I tried to keep track of where I went, but I was soon lost among the dead. There was no one I could ask about my father. To know for the rest of my life that this is where he would lie for the rest of his.

I found lots of fathers, but no father of mine, and then waiting until the moon appeared to read names. I read lots of dates, but no dates that matched his. Now I was carrying all the gravestones in my head, counting them and searching them again in case I'd missed something, I must have, I was angry at myself that I never came here. I fingered the pills and slipped one into my mouth. It raced my heart to my head.

The rain came down. It fell everywhere from the sky over the graveyard. And mixed into it I saw refrigerators, cribs, houses, wind, syringes, crystals, streets, windows, swirling, funneling down over the stones on the wide lawns, soaring, dipping, littering the sky, drops driven together into faces and those faces torn up by wind and driven separately into the ground.

The tiredness was doing it, making faces out of raindrops. Making things from a life all appear together without a past or present to separate them. Sleep would drive those images away.

What a thing, to be lost among the dead. I smiled and did not know why. Someone should live in a little house in the cemetery, someone who lives in candlelight so that you can see his shadow and knock on his door if you need directions, that is if he doesn't see you first and comes to help, dragging a coat over the shadow of his running frame, a keeper of graves. He manages the graveyard and lives among the dead and therefore must by law also know the history of each person buried in the cemetery, remember those he never knew. And when schoolchildren come to visit out of yellow school buses he brings them to a grave and says, Here is Johnny Armstrong who died in 1986. Let me tell you about where he grew up and who his friends were. His known relatives have died and I am the only person who remembers. I carry this knowledge.

Why were the dead buried anyway? Below ground, the dead were invisible twice. Gone from your life and gone from theirs. And how long should a body stay in a graveyard when no one visits anymore, why keep a grave? And what was the order of burial—by date alone? They could reserve sections for men, for women, for boys and girls, or by profession: for lawyers, professors, truck drivers. Or they could divide up the plots according to people's inclinations: for the depressed, the joyful, optimists, pessimists, the jealous, the spiteful, the wistful, the remorseful, the stoics. But the best way entirely might be none of the above.

Why not bury according to the number of friends a person had? Those with many friends and acquaintances could be placed closer to the road, easier to visit. Those with fewer friends could be buried off into the middle where those few could come looking for them. And finally, by the extreme far walls in the undergrowth, the section for recluses: their privacy continued into death.

Create a city of the dead. You walk the corridors of this city—the alleys, the parks—and you find the dead above the ground. They sit in chairs, they stand in doorways, they look out at the sea. You shop for bread with the dead stacked everywhere around you.

If I could know the date of my own death from the moment of my birth, if I could live like Andy and know the time of my death but not where I was born, I could live toward my beginning, not my end. I could have enough experience to know what to do when I was young. But would I live any better? My brother must have been tired growing up with me, without a body, always having to follow me, with nowhere for him. What could I have done for him? There was one thing.

I closed my eyes and opened the door to the dark he lived in and let him go.

Yes, this was the place, my father's grave. A stone with his name. I sat on the grass for a minute and looked around at the neat lines. The rain was over, the clouds thinner, the moon, that's what it was, a moon, sailing behind them, clear in the loose threads. I tore out the prescription for Elevax and pressed it to his stone. Can you read this? This is the person I became after you.

I checked the graves on each side and did not recognize the names. I wondered if my father had ever passed in life the strangers lying beside him in this place, passed them on the street, sat beside them in a movie, swayed to somewhere in the same bus.

For such a still place, the graveyard was complicated: graves, monuments, flowerbeds, statues, a litter of memory and not a sound but my breath, the only breath here. I passed under trees past poems and pictures wrapped in plastic and pinned to the stone against the weather. A drawing a child made. A key. A pair of shoes wrapped in twine. A button. A wine glass.

If I saw my mother again in the future, or saw my father too, if one day I did see them, what age would they be? The age they were when they got married, or would their ages be different? Would my father look like he did when he was sick and my mother when she was young? If people did go to an afterlife, what age were they there?

My head was clear, the weather blowing away the pills. They did not take. I lost the dreams in them when my head blew clear. The graves were the antidote. No one in a graveyard takes a pill. They do not work here. That must be why.

But I wanted the dream, I wanted the feeling my father had at this moment, I wanted to see what he saw at this moment. I wanted the graveyard to go away.

So I took the rest of them, all of them. And Fargoon's Elevax. I opened my mouth to the rain to help them down.

I walked the lines of stones and wondered how much more a child could know of a mother and father. Their friends knew them as much as I did. I came to a stretch of new graves, and of course the moon went under a cloud and I had to bend close to the stones to read them, even running my fingers along the carved names. And then I was back at my father's grave. Something I had not noticed before, a shadow across it. Or the moon had moved. I looked up and saw the figure that blocked its light, the shadow of raindrop wings holding a sword. The sword was loose in the hand, the eyes were open. It was the fly.

I sat for a while against his gravestone, waiting for what came next. The pills came for me at last, the floating of a dream that skims the surface of the mind and sinks in. The cold went away, the cold stone of my father went away. How quickly they all worked together. I thought of Swan, thought of him on that long flight back to the carrier ship in the dark, his friends waiting for him. He would be the last to land on that mowed lawn, the last to get his flag hoisted in the breeze and his melody played, and before that day came the only thing left to fight was his breath. Meanwhile his friends whisper from the grass, I was twenty, I was twenty-three. Let me tell you my story.

I could have been friends with Mr. Swan.

I was warm now. But this was a bigger blanket than I had known in my life. It found my eyes and sank to my mouth, swelled it and freed it from feeling, it trickled down to my jaw and made it senseless. A sprinkle of pills in my right and left eyes, a few along the lips, five or six stuffed into each ear, a small pile on my right breast, another on my left, pills on my right hand and pills on my left, a few more in the pockets in case there was an afterlife and I ran out. They moved down to my throat, my throat swelled and no words would come from it.

Across the path under the shadow of the fly's wings there was a smaller, temporary stone, the type they use until the clay underneath settles. I dragged myself closer, or else it moved toward me slowly until I reached it.

Although Mr. Swan was wrong, I lay on my back above her, in case it was her. Now we were together, all of us again. I imagined her lying under me. I watched the clouds race light across the night and across the cemetery. I took off the coat, the sweater, the shirt, and lay again. I closed my eyes and waited to feel something, turned face down until the warm swilled down to my stomach and my sight sank down with it.

I lost my sight. That meant the night was inside me. I said, Mother.

I waited for the echo to come back to me. The word came back from under the ground. I closed my eyes fully and made claws of my hands, scraped the earth until it tore away to harder clay and small stones. When the clay filled my hands I knew I could go farther, and I dug faster, shoulder first. When I reached the wood I took a stone and battered it. Such dark down there, and the moon was hidden behind my body, but splinters of light cut into the coffin, and I saw her face. I lay on top of her. I moved aside her skin and her ribs, I found her lungs, moved them aside and saw her womb. I should lie on her and try to warm her. Then I took her heart, still beating, and held it to my face, held it there and felt it beat.

I said, Where are you?

I found an arm, a hand that combed my hair, the face that looked at mine when I was born.

Her name was Mary. She lay in the trickle of the moon through the clay, her eyes closed, skin drawn tight. The thin gray hair rested on the pillow, her shape bent in sleep like a broken coat hanger. I had never seen skin like that, bruised and drained, a pile of gray rock. I wanted to look away but no room. Her hands, joined over her chest, straws with bones inside. I remembered her hand, one knuckle at a time. The knuckle of her index finger. She trailed that finger along my forehead one day. I was very young, so young I smelled her finger more than saw it. Her second finger. I was older and lay in bed on a Saturday morning and she massaged my arms while she read me a story. Her skin like honey and the fresh linen of the blue and white bedcovers. The sun came in the window but stayed in a corner where it heated the room like a bright chair. Her third finger. She wrapped the wool around it when she knitted, once I watched while she made me a pair of gloves. I watched the needles criss-cross and the single spool of string dart left and right, coming out the other side in a wall of red shaping into a glove, I called it magic. She liked that and shook her head and smiled at the same time, her head was knitting too.

From inside her the pills finally walked out to the

edge of her skin, walked out of her ears with their hands up, they must have heard the word I called.

Secanol and Lorazepam, they say.

Which one of you killed my mother?

They speak, they have no choice: She took all of us.

The Elixir of Aprobarbital sneaks out beside them. We couldn't do anything.

I never saw you in the house, I say.

What else do you not know about your own mother, they say. We live in containers, in all manner of them, in jars, in pillows, in pockets, in the memory, in what people forget. But your mother, she could not forget. That was her disease.

In this way I heard them singing through the grains of the clay to me, the worlds of clay, holding forth in her coffin. The ones inside her and inside me stood in a line and spelled my name before my closed eyes, half the letters in me and half in her, and those bits of letters were my name, but I had no light in me, they never gave me light, and I in turn carried nothing down the stalk to her, I never gave her anything in my life.

The heat I felt now suddenly must have been my father and mother: they were both inside me for the first time because they were gone for the first time. They were gone and I felt them more than before. I could keep them in me for ever. Wait. I needed to remember. There was the lake, there was the crib. My father, my mother, my brother. There was the bird I loved and did not know why. I must remember, know they are inside me. Too late, the pills had melted their names into my blood, did their job and disappeared, swam to my head in the red stream, and now it was my turn to dissolve.

And it was cold, it was cold. I lay above her. My heart tolled once, told me it had not beat for a minute. I said that living was cold, not to bother again. It did not answer. The thoughts in my head became one: the slow Blue Jay in the garden with the seeds and the lines around his saucer eyes before he died on his own and was lost. How I cried. Then some part of the sun must have found me, it looked up from me, or it was me who looked up from my mother's body and down into the sky, and when I saw no light, I looked down more for her, down into the stars.

ACKNOWLEDGEMENTS

Thanks to Jin Auh, my agent; to David Shoemaker, my editor, whose sense for what I do makes what I do better; to Jay Prefontaine and Celeste DeSario for their reading; and to Peter Mayer for publishing this novel in the United States.